INTERSECTIONS

SHANELLE O. BOLUYT

FIFTH
AVENUE
PRESS

Intersections

Fifth Avenue Press is a locally focused and publicly owned publishing imprint of the Ann Arbor District Library. It is dedicated to supporting the local writing community by promoting the production of original fiction, non-fiction and poetry written for children, teens and adults.

Printed in the United States of America

First Printing, 2019

Cover Illustration: Kirbi Fagan

Layout: Ann Arbor District Library

ISBN: 978-1-947989-57-3 (Hardcover); ISBN: 978-1-947989-58-0 (Paperback); ISBN: 978-1-947989-59-7 (Ebook)

For my Family

CHARACTERS

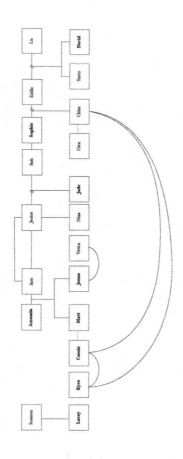

THE END

This is what you will remember:
Blinding sun
Falling from a pyramid
Grass-stained knees
Giggling voices
Shiny new car
Taunting, teasing
A sudden stop
The world tilting
Falling
Shattering sounds
Voices
What happened?
How are you?
Chloe!
Talk to me!
I love you
It's going to be OK; I love you; please be OK
Darkness

1

ECHOES

When I can't sleep at night, I watch CNN. This has happened pretty much every night for the last month, every night since the accident, every night since Chloe died.

The first night, my mom sat up with me.

"We should watch something less . . . boring, David," she said. She ran a fingernail along the threadbare arm of the sofa.

"They're dropping bombs in the Middle East," I told her. I sat hunched forward, chin resting in my hands. This was important, I told myself. This was what I needed to pay attention to.

"Something happy," my mother said.

She used to be over there, in the Middle East. She had signed up thinking the National Guard would help pay the bills, but then she got sent over there to fix tanks. She came back kind of wobbly and doesn't like to leave the house much.

Travis, my brother, says she went over there wobbly, and just came back worse.

I felt bad for her and changed the channel. We watched SpongeBob try to win some fry cook competition, then switched over to an actual fry cook competition on the Food Network.

When it got really late, the infomercials took over and she muted the TV.

"You should really sleep," she said.

I shrugged.

She got up and came back a few minutes later with a white pill and some water. "Trazodone," she said. "It's completely safe."

She looked tired, so I took it.

Fifteen minutes into a very tempting offer on the Ninja food processor, I slipped out of consciousness.

I woke up sometime in the middle of the night to pee and found I could barely stand. With my sweat-soaked hand pressed against the wall, I felt myself slide to the bathroom floor. I woke up sometime later, my face pressed against the cool tile and dragged myself back to the worn blue plaid couch.

I turned the TV back on and watched CNN, and then lost consciousness again.

All night, drifting through my dreams, I heard her whimpering.

After that, I pretend to take the Trazodone when my mother hands it to me, then pocket it. I save them up and trade four of them for a dime bag at school.

I wave her off when she offers to stay up and tell her I'll be asleep soon. Then I turn on CNN.

There is always, without fail, something happening. A child missing, a murder, earthquakes, tornadoes, tsunamis, floods, wars.

Tonight the top story is about two young Boy Scouts who have gone missing up in Muskegon. That's where we used to camp. My father would come up every summer, from wherever he was living, and take us up there for a week or two. Me, Travis, and Chloe, our half-sister.

When we were little kids and I would see her at school, I would point her out to my friends. "Look, there's my sister." I didn't think there was anything weird about it, even though we didn't live together. She must have said something similar, because once or twice I ran into one of her friends and they said something like, "Oh, you're Chloe's brother, right?"

We kind of looked alike. Her hair was curly and mine was short, but they were the same dark brown. Our eyes were both dark blue, like our father's. We both had a bit of a bump on the bridge of our noses that you wouldn't notice unless you looked at us real close.

The Boy Scouts have been missing since yesterday afternoon. Fell behind on a hike and haven't been seen since. The hike was through some "trails" that weren't really maintained, "off the beaten path," as their Scout Master keeps putting it. By the time the Scout Master noticed the kids were missing, the sun was setting, and there was no hope of him leading the volunteer search party along their path. They've looked around the perimeter, and are "relying on the boys' survival skills training" to keep them alive through the night.

I'm thinking the Scout Master gets fired after this. Assuming it's a paid position. He's probably a volunteer, and possibly a perv—there was a story on that last week, on the Boy Scouts covering it up like the priests, and CNN re-ran it about once an hour to ensure full saturation. They called it a "developing story," but nothing new seemed to develop. Then a politician got caught sexting an underage intern, and the news moved on.

The missing Scouts story is "breaking news." If they're not found in the morning, the story will heat up, will be covered round the clock, to the exclusion of all else. Then tomorrow evening, another story will break in, just for a couple of minutes, and, within a week, everyone will lose interest, and the story will be dropped.

Of course, for their parents, for their brothers and sisters and grandparents and best friends, the story will never go away. The news vans will turn tail and leave, but the story will hang over them, a rumbling cloud, an unanswered question, a deep well in which to drown. While the world moves on, their lives will be haunted, tortured. They will go from living to surviving, if they even make it that far.

Right now, they're all thinking about the last things they said to the kids. Or, if they can't remember that, they're trying to figure out what it was, and thinking about the last *mean* thing they said. And hating themselves.

I can imagine how much worse it will get, if they don't find the boys.

I think of the Scouts as they must be now: cold, scared, tired. If they survive, this will become a cool adventure, a great story, the time they were on CNN. Their families will be happier than they ever thought possible. But right now, the boys are just terrified. They are curled up in the leaves, waiting for a search party that won't be useful until the morning, hearing every sound—the coyote's howls, the vulture's screech, even just the spring leaves rustling in the wind—as a threat, a danger, coming for them.

They will hear other things, too. The thundering crashes of the waves on the lake's shore (maybe they can follow this sound to rescue?), the buzzy electric sound of the cicadas (or is it too late in the year for them?), the popping, rattling sound of the campfire's dying breath (or did they not remember how to build one?). These were the sounds Chloe and I would hear when we would slip out for our nightly trek to the beach.

"The ocean," we called it, even though it wasn't. But there were waves and a beach and water that went on endlessly. Anything could be at the other end. Or nothing at all.

It was best at night, when all of the tourists had gone to bed. When we had the place to ourselves. We would slip out of our sleeping bags, tiptoeing and shushing each other, holding in our breaths while we unzipped the tent, careful not to wake Travis.

Then we would run as best we could up the sand dune, feet sinking with every step. Over the crest, we would tumble down the hill, falling half a dozen times as we raced toward the water.

It was too cold at night to swim, so we would just wade in, feeling the gentle tug of the waves as they wrapped themselves around our ankles.

When we got tired of that, we chased each other up and down the dunes and shrieked as loud as we could—there was no one to hear. We played tag by moonlight and searched for treasures. When we'd spent our energy, we lay back on the dunes and made up constellations—the Unicorn, the Spiderman, the Rusted-out Impala.

"One day I'm going to live here," Chloe said once. "You can come visit me sometime."

"You have to have a lot of money to live here," I told her.

"I'm going to be rich," she said, chin jutted upward, eyes sparkling in the moonlight. "I'm going to have a mansion and a chauffeur, and ride around in a swimming pool in my limousine."

"You're crazy," I said. "What are you going to do to get rich?"

"I'll be an actress," she declared, throwing out her arms and spinning. Her dark curls twirled in the moonlight.

"Most actresses are really waitresses," I said.

She rolled her eyes. "You're so depressing," she said. "My mom says I can totally make it as an actress. Or a doctor, though they don't make as much money. Maybe a brain doctor; she says they make a lot."

"You need a lot of money to be a brain doctor," I told her. "College and then more college and then other stuff."

"You don't need anything to be an actress," she said. "Just talent."

"As if you have talent," I said.

"Shut up," she said, shoving me lightly. "My mom says I am very talented at 'spinning tales that deviate from the truth.' She also says I know how to get people to do what I want."

"She's saying you know how to lie and use people."

She shook her head. "I can use my talent for good or evil. I choose to use it for good. I will entertain the world and make a million dollars."

"Sure you will."

"You're just jealous because you have no talents," she said.

"For your information, I am very good at lying around and not doing anything."

She threw back her head, her high-pitched giggle mingling with the crashing of the waves.

She'll never live on the beach now. She'll never live anywhere.

I wonder if she had still wanted to be an actress, or if she had moved on to something else, something more real.

In my mind, she is frozen at age eleven, the last time we were really friends.

For the last few years it's felt like she was out there, in a parallel universe. I would catch glimpses of her, at school, as if looking through some magical glass portal where I could see her, but never quite know what she was saying. I watched her live her life, watched her grow older. Prancing about in a cheerleader uniform. Cartwheeling down the hall on the last day of school. Laughing at lunch with her friends.

It was nice to know I could just look through that glass and see she was OK.

My older brother, Travis, comes downstairs at two in the morning, which is something he does sometimes.

"You should be sleeping," he says.

"Boy Scouts are missing," I tell him. I run my hand across my chin. I haven't shaved in at least a week, but all I can feel are a few stray hairs.

"Somebody's always missing," he says.

I shrug.

"Why the hell do you watch this stuff?"

I shrug again. I can't really explain it. It's just so much more real than everything else on TV.

"You're going to turn into one of those old men who shakes his fist at the TV and says the world is going to hell."

"What's wrong with that?"

He rolls his eyes and drops onto the couch, grabbing a half-eaten box of Cheez-Its from the floor.

"Old people have wisdom and whatnot."

"Old people like to bitch," he says.

"You like to bitch."

"Yeah, well, I'm old."

"Whatever," I say. He's five years older than me. Just barely able to legally drink.

CNN flashes a photo of the boys in their uniforms on the screen. The words "MISSING BOY SCOUTS" appear below.

"We used to go camping up there," I say.

"Yeah, back when Dad pretended to make an effort."

I shrug. "He took me out for burgers last week."

"Oh, great. Did you supersize it? Because that would totally make up for, what, three, four years of no contact."

"He sent birthday cards."

"Two weeks late."

One time. Other times they were only a couple of days late. But I don't feel like arguing.

Travis was the one who called him, after we got back from the hospital. I couldn't, and Chloe's mom, Sophie, couldn't, so Travis did.

"This is depressing," Travis says. He reaches for the

remote that's sitting between us and I let him take it. He switches the channel a couple of times until he finds an old episode of *The Simpsons*.

"Are you taking the pills Mom gives you?" he asks.

"No."

"That's probably a good thing. You don't want to end up like her."

"I thought she was like that because she doesn't take the pills."

He shrugs his shoulders.

"What do you do with the pills?" he asks after a minute. When I don't answer, he says, "You can't go around selling that shit. You'll end up in juvie or something."

"I don't sell it," I say.

He looks at me for a minute.

"Trading is not the same as selling," I say. Unlike Chloe, I am no good at lying.

"Christ," he says, massaging his forehead with his palm. "You all think nothing bad is ever going to happen. Even my crappy-ass job won't hire you if you have a felony. And you'd be surprised what counts as a felony."

I sort of doubt it's really a felony, but I don't want to argue, and I figure I can just give it to Jade next time, and she can handle things from there. Sort of a gift for all the times I've bummed weed off her. If she trades it for weed and I bum more off her . . . well, that's not a crime.

"Whatever," I say. "I won't trade it anymore."

He looks at me again, decides I'm not lying, and goes back to the TV.

"Do you think Chloe still wanted to be an actress?" I ask. Everything freezes until I remember to breathe.

"Fuck," he says.

Then he doesn't say anything for a while. Bart chases Lisa around the living room while Homer bitches at them to stop blocking the TV.

"Probably not," he says finally. "People grow up."

"She thought she was going to be rich."

"Everyone thinks they're going to be rich when they're young. It's the TV and the schools and whatever. They tell you that you can be whatever the hell you want."

"I never thought I was going to be rich."

"Yeah, well, you were always depressing."

"Realistic," I say.

"Reality is depressing," he says. "Why do you think you smoke so much pot?"

I laugh, and he looks at me with a sigh and a kind of half-smile, because it shouldn't really be funny.

He falls asleep before the end credits. I nudge him with my elbow and tell him to go back to bed.

"You should get some sleep," he mutters as he heads up the stairs.

"Soon," I say.

Like a moth drawn to the twisting, shimmering flame, I turn back to CNN.

They have nothing new to report; after all, they've "suspended search operations" until the morning, so they are filling time with interviews and prognostication.

The family is too upset to talk, so they have settled for the Scout Master, who keeps saying things like, "The boys have their training, they'll be fine," which sounds like wishful thinking to me. Every so often, CNN gets a statement from the police. It's never anything new, but they have a count-down to it and everything. When they get tired of talking about what the latest report means, they move on to a choppy phone interview with a fifteen-year-old kid, another Boy Scout, who went missing at thirteen and survived for three days.

These boys are eleven.

. . .

The summer we were eleven sticks out in my mind. Or I was ten. Chloe would have been eleven; she was always older in the summer. It was not until mid-October that we would be the same age again.

In a week, I will be sixteen, just like her.

Next October, if I make it that long, I will be older than her. From then on, I will be forever older than her. She will be frozen in time, gone missing from the parallel universe, and I will keep getting older without her.

But in the summers, she was always older than me. She was older, but when I would ask our dad for money, he would scrunch up his face at me and ask, "What did you do to earn it?" and when she would ask, he would always say, "Sure, princess, how much do you need?"

She would always get enough for both of us, and we would slip away and run the mile to the edge of the campground, where scraggly grass grew around the dirty sand, to the stand that sold ice cream and popsicles, candy sticks and Laffy Taffy. We would blow it all right there, an ice cream each—three scoops—and a mixed bag of candy to share.

We would linger to eat the ice cream. There was a single picnic table in front of the stand, and if it was unoccupied, we would sit there, licking our rapidly melting ice cream cones and divvying up the candy through various games of chance and skill. Rock-paper-scissors to see who would pick first. Then a dare issued, like, if you run over and lick that tree, you can pick two pieces. If you let that spider crawl up your arm, you can get three turns in a row. If you ask the guy who's working the stand if he wears boxers or briefs, you can have the Reese's and I'll pick something else.

After the candy was divided and the last of the ice cream slurped, we would begin trading, fingers sticky from melted mint chocolate chip and butter rum. Because, of course, you didn't just pick the candy you wanted most. Sometimes you picked the kind the other one liked. So you could trade.

What can I say? The campground didn't have TV, and we had time to kill. We didn't really want to go back to the campsite, where Travis was always saying something snarky to our father, or our father was screaming at Travis.

One time our father grabbed Travis's shirt, like he was going to punch him, before he stopped himself and stormed off into the woods and didn't come back until long after the sun had set.

We ate candy for dinner that night.

Before the accident, Jade used to eat lunch with her cousin Matt and another guy. They were all in a band together. I used to sit with the burnouts and not say much, which was fine, because half the guys were staring into space. The other half were just amazed by the layers in the sandwich or how a burrito "came to be."

After everything, Jade stopped sitting with her cousin. She picked a table in the middle of the cafeteria and motioned for me to sit with her. We were upgraded from detention friends to lunch friends.

She got the new girl, Lacey, sitting with us too.

They were both there that day. Every time I think about it I feel like there is a black hole in my gut, sucking everything toward it.

Jade talked a lot, though, so that filled the space. And she was nice to look at, zippers all over her clothes, sometimes unzipped, sometimes showing a flash of skin beneath. She's short and curvy and likes to do crazy beautiful things with her hair.

"I think I want to live in New York," she said one day. Her hair was slashed with green and pink streaks, two small clusters of it twisted into buns that vaguely resembled alien eyes.

"New York is expensive," I told her. I stabbed my fries into a cup of ranch.

"Not if you do it right. There are all these, like, panhandlers who can actually afford apartments, like, *nice* apartments, off of what they make. I just need a talent or to paint myself green or something."

"Living art," Lacey said.

"Exactly."

"Didn't Giuliani kick all the panhandlers out?"

"He kicked out the homeless people pissing in alleyways, not the panhandlers with apartments," Jade said. "And I could always live in Chicago."

I silently predicted she would go to college (because her mother had money), get kicked out (because she's Jade), and end up living in her mom's basement, working at the used video game store (slash tanning salon) until they replace it with a website and the sun.

"I used to live near Chicago," Lacey said.

Jade turned her full attention on Lacey, her metal-clad eyebrow arched. "I thought you said you lived in some nothing town. You've been holding out on us. What was it like?"

"Well, I mean, I didn't live *in* the city. I lived in the suburbs."

"I totally pictured you living in the cornfields or something. You were city-adjacent, though. You must have gone there all the time."

"Museums for school trips and things like that."

"That's lame."

Lacey shrugged. "My mom took me to the free zoo a few times. I saw the beach there once. And my friend's mom took us to this really cool area on Belmont. They had tattoo parlors and really neat clothing shops and record stores and all sorts of weird food, like an Asian taco bar."

"That's where I want to be," Jade said. "I want to eat Asian tacos and work in a tattoo parlor."

"I thought you wanted to panhandle?" I asked.

She shrugged. "I don't know what I'll do. I'll figure it out when I get there."

"You could go now," I said. I don't know why I said it. Sometimes I just say things.

Lacey narrowed her brown eyes at me, as if to say, *What are you doing? Don't let her leave us.*

"My mom would probably send the National Guard out after me," Jade said.

I kind of doubted it. Last year, Jade estimated she spent over a hundred days couch hopping. Her mother never seemed too bothered by it.

"They're not going to find you in the city, though," I said.

Lacey continued to glare.

"Maybe," Jade said. Her mouth twisted around. "I can't leave now, anyway," she said. "Sophie needs me."

My insides twisted.

Sophie was Chloe's mother. My dad's former mistress. Jade's stepmother, more-or-less (Jade's father had been living with Sophie for years). But she was nothing to me, really.

The whole reason Jade and I were ever sort of friends was that we used to swap rumors and stories about Chloe. Nothing over the top, but nothing all that nice, either. Then I started bumming weed off her, and since her mother had money, she didn't have a problem sharing.

"You should really stop by and visit her," Jade said.

Lacey looked back and forth between us, trying to figure out what was going on.

"I have nothing to say to her."

"Seriously?"

"What do you say to her? 'Oh, hey, remember that time Chloe was all upset because someone wrote *Fake* on her locker? That was us.'"

Lacey opened her mouth like she wanted to say something, then closed it.

Jade rolled her eyes. "That was kid stuff. She did stuff to us, too. None of it matters now."

"Right," I said. "Because it's how you treat people when they're dead that really matters. Not how you treated them when they were alive."

"You know what," Jade said, her dark eyes opened wide, "you are being a real dick right now." She took a breath. "Don't worry, I forgive you. You want to come get high later, you find me. C'mon." She stood, whipping her shimmering hair around as she jerked her face away from me. "I think I'm done with lunch."

Lacey, who still had three-quarters of her sandwich left, also stood, shooting me a weird, scrunched-up look.

After they left, I found that I, too, had lost my appetite.

On CNN, they manage to get an uncle to talk to them. He issues a "statement" about how they'd like to thank the volunteers on the search party, and how the families are holding up because they have faith in the boys' training and faith in God.

The families are not holding up, I can tell you that much. Everyone lies about that stuff.

Once a week, the guidance counselor pulls me into her office to ask me how I'm doing. I sit in her closet of an office and look at her across her desk and tell her I'm fine. That I barely even knew Chloe. That I'm doing OK. That I'm falling asleep in class because it's boring, not because I'm sitting up at night, every night, watching CNN.

That next summer, when I was eleven, just before we left for the beach, I asked my brother why he and my dad fought so much. Everything, I thought, would be so much better if Travis just shut up and let us all be happy.

"Dad's a bastard," he said.

"No, he's not," I said, my debating skills severely limited.

"You don't know anything," Travis said.

I stared at him and waited. Travis had always loved imparting everything he knew.

"Do the math," he said. "I love Chloe, she's a hell of a lot less annoying than you, but do the math. It takes nine months to make a baby, and even if it didn't, she's older than you. Dad was married to Mom. Think about it. Dad's a bastard," he repeated. "Well, technically Chloe is, but she didn't exactly ask to be born."

I didn't have to think too much about it. I was no stranger to *Springer*.

"OK," I said, trying to act like I had done the math a long time ago. I felt like an idiot. I had never really given the fact that I had a sister about my own age much thought, other than: *Oh, cool*.

"Did Mom know?" I asked finally.

"I don't think at first, but I think Sophie told her at some point . . . it was never the same after that. You know, Mom and Dad were happy once. She used to dance around the kitchen. She'd friggin' sing. She was totally off key and I was always yelling at her to stop, but she didn't care. She would go to work and make dinner and all of that normal stuff. And we had money, not a lot, but we didn't have to take food stamps. He would come home from work, and we would all eat dinner and watch *The Simpsons* and they would both laugh. All the time. Almost every night. He screwed everything up."

I figured Travis probably knew just as long as Mom had—he was smart like that. But I was too young to even remember the times my dad lived with us—he stayed with us when our mom was overseas, but he always left the moment she came back. So I had always figured this was normal. He was a treat, when we saw him. Something mythical that we had to share with Chloe, and maybe with others, too.

I had never really thought that it was supposed to be different, that we were supposed to have him all the time.

"Did Sophie know?" I asked.

"That she was sleeping with a married man?" he asked. "Of course she knows. She knew. I don't really blame her, though. She was nineteen; she was young and stupid. She didn't know. She didn't know Mom or me. You didn't even exist yet. She didn't know what she was destroying."

I didn't say anything, just nodded solemnly and tried to look smart.

I wish I had just stayed dumb forever.

Chloe was twelve and starting to morph into a teenager. I was eleven and still just a kid. Chloe was starting to get moody. She'd stop in the middle of a game of tag and say, "This is stupid." When I found a half-smoked cigarette and tried to light it, she said, "You shouldn't smoke that. It could have AIDS."

I dared her to smoke it, but she just rolled her eyes and walked off.

The third day of camping, we were sitting at a picnic table, divvying up our candy when I dared her to eat a bug. Not a big one, just a little mosquito I had killed.

"Ew, that's disgusting," she said. "No way."

"Fine," I said. "Then it's my pick, and I'll take the Reese's."

"Whatever," she said, cocking her head upward and running a chipped pink fingernail through her hair. "This is stupid. All this candy is mine anyway. Dad gave me the money, not you."

With a swipe, she pulled all of the candy toward her, mine and hers, and into the brown paper bag.

"That's not fair!" I said.

"Yes, it is. It's *my* money."

"You're not even the real kid, you're just the bastard!" I spat out.

She had been looking down, at the bag full of candy, and she kept her face angled down, but her dark blue eyes jutted up at me, wide and open. Just staring.

"Your mom's a slut," I added.

She rolled up the top of the bag and stood. She started to walk away, then turned back and looked at me, eyes still wide as a full moon. "He must not have loved your mom," she said quietly. "And he obviously doesn't love you."

I stood up with a jerk and ran at her. She turned but I shoved her anyway. She fell into the sandy grass, the bag falling in front of her, a Reese's spilling out.

She turned to look up at me with her big owl eyes.

She said nothing.

I thought about taking the bag. Or just the Reese's.

In the end, I just ran.

When I found her back at the campsite an hour later, neither of us said a word.

The next summer, just before we were set to leave on our trip, she said she was sick. A flu or a bad cold or something. My dad cancelled the trip.

We never went back.

When I would see her in the halls at school, I wouldn't wave. I didn't point her out, didn't say, "That's my sister."

She came over to the house sometimes, to talk to Travis. To complain about her mother, to ask for a ride to the mall, and the last time, to cry about getting drunk and sleeping with her boyfriend or something.

"So I guess she got drunk and slept with him. I don't get why it's a big deal," I told Jade while we shared a joint in the bathroom during detention. Since she provided the weed, I had to both venture into the women's room and cough up information. "And she hasn't told anyone, because she's so *ashamed*."

"Well, of course," Jade said. "She's Little Miss Sunday School. She has a fucking promise ring. If she pisses me off this week, I'm going to totally write her a note. *I know what you did last Friday.* Was it last Friday? It's kind of important that I get the date right. Of course, *I know what you did two Fridays ago,* really doesn't have the same punch. Please tell me it was last Friday. Or Saturday or whatever."

"I think it was a few weeks ago," I said, rolling my eyes and putting out my hand for the joint.

"Damn," Jade muttered.

Then some freshman ran into the bathroom, hyperventilating.

"There's been an accident!" she screamed. "Right at the corner." She looked at us. "What are you doing in here? Wait, are you guys getting high?"

We walked past her and out the door. We were drawn to the accident by some invisible force. To gawk at other people's misery. To catch some of the excitement. To have an excuse not to return to detention.

I recognized the car right away. A brand-new shiny silver shrunken car, the kind of car that talks to your smart phone and costs three hundred dollars a month, maybe more. Cassie's car. Chloe's best friend's car. Spun around in the middle of the intersection, the passenger side caved in. People were screaming.

I was silent. I was running.

Chloe always rode with Cassie.

On TV, the Breaking News is that the Scouts wandered back into camp. They're cold and tired and hungry and perfectly fine.

Everyone can resume their regularly scheduled lives.

The room starts to brighten with the sun's rise, the outline of the TV and entertainment stand becoming clearer. I let myself drift, just a bit, toward the great undertow of slumber.

When I jerk awake, the sound of Chloe's moaning rings in my ears. In the street where I found her lying on the stretcher, looking up past me with wide white eyes, like I wasn't even there. Screaming, but almost silently, because there wasn't enough breath in her for anything louder. Screaming, moaning, her eyes already gone blank.

And then there wasn't any breath in her anymore, and she was silent.

I know she didn't really die in that moment; it was an hour later on some sterilized white operating table, walled off from anyone who ever loved her, but this is what I remember.

I remember bending over her as they prepared to load her into the ambulance.

I remember her eyes, looking at nothing. Her quiet moaning, her almost screaming.

I remember the sound of her last breath.

And I remember the silence after, deafening.

The only thing worse than the silence is the other sound I wake to some nights. The echo of her choked sobs, muffled within the sleeping bag, after she thought I had fallen asleep that night in Muskegon. The thick sound of her breathing in, the shaky sound as the breath left her body.

When I wake up to that, I turn the volume all the way up on CNN, so loud it shakes the ceiling and maybe even wakes Travis. But it's never loud enough. The sounds of her sobs ring in my ears all night.

2

WHAT IS, WHAT WAS, AND WHAT WILL NEVER BE

Some people didn't get why we were friends.

Chloe was the cheerleader-and-bake-sale kind of girl. Always peppy, always up. Always running around hugging people. Everybody loved Chloe.

Cassie was the straight-A, type-A little go-getter. Smart, driven, cutting through conversations with no time for niceties, like she was in a race or something.

And I—Kyra—was the jock. I'd rather be drenched in sweat than doing my nails. I'd sooner knock you on your ass than give you hug.

Some people didn't get why the three of us were friends, but it made sense to me. We were each the best, we kicked ass, we always came out on top. If we were all into the same thing, we probably would have killed each other.

With three of us, everything sort of balanced out.

But now there are only two.

———

It always used to be like this:

CHLOE

So then Glen was all, "I don't know what the big deal is," and
I was like, "I don't want to drag you home drunk," and he
was all—

CASSIE

Why the hell do you put up with him?

CHLOE

He's pretty.

CASSIE

That's a really stupid reason to put up with that crap.

ME (a.k.a. KYRA)

Yes, and Matt's just perfect.

CASSIE

At least he treats me right.

CHLOE

Glen can be really great. Guess what he did for my birthday . .
.

ME

I don't think Matt even *remembered* Cassie's birthday.

CASSIE

He remembered it.

ME

Didn't you add it to his phone?

CASSIE

So?

CHLOE

So that's not the same as remembering it.

CASSIE

Whatever. He would have remembered it.

ME

Sure.

———

Cassie doesn't call me after the accident.

They'd taken us to the hospital to get checked out. I'm guessing Cassie wasn't in for long. All she broke was her nose.

I broke my leg, so it took a few hours.

My dad came in after a little bit. He already knew. He's a cop, so I wonder if he knew before everyone else. I'm sure they said things, the guys on the scene. Like how she probably wasn't going to make it.

I didn't suspect it, though. I was stupid and thought we were all going to be OK, except for maybe Cassie's new car.

I had been in too much pain to really see anything. Chloe had been lying on me for a bit, I think, but I remember feeling her breath against my ear, so I assumed she was OK. She rode in the other ambulance, so I tried asking Cassie about her on the ride to the hospital, but she was just breathing in and out, in and out, like someone having a baby, twisting her shoulder-length dark hair between her fingers.

That should have been a sign.

The way my dad looked when he came into the room— pale face drawn, gaze averted—that should have been another sign.

I made a joke about how my leg looked worse than it felt, thanks to the morphine.

And then he started crying.

Anyway, after that, everything is different.

Cassie doesn't call me. I keep expecting her to show up —*her* leg isn't broken. She always used to come over when she was upset.

Or go to Chloe's.

But she doesn't come. I lay in bed and text "R U OK?" and she doesn't reply.

I take a Vicodin and sleep.

———

CASSIE

Guess what?!

ME

You found out you're adopted and your parents just made up the whole unwanted pregnancy thing to scare you off from having sex?

CHLOE

You discovered what they actually put in the meat at Taco Bell?

CASSIE

I'm getting a car!!!!

ME

No way your parents can afford to buy you a car.

CASSIE

No, dummy, *I'm* buying me a car.

CHLOE

You make enough for that?

CASSIE

It's a cute little car. The payments are only three hundred a month. I can make that in a good weekend.

CHLOE

OMG, that is so awesome. You're totally giving us rides everywhere.

CASSIE

Duh.

ME

Why would you want to spend that kind of money on a *car*?

CHLOE

Ignore her. She's just jealous you passed your road test. This is going to be totally awesome.

———

I was too young when my mother died to remember her funeral. So Chloe's is basically my first.

Goddamn, it's depressing.

People get up and speak. Cassie gets up and speaks. She wears a long black dress that definitely does not pop against her dark skin and wears silver barrettes to keep her black hair out of her face. Her eyes have dark crescent moons beneath them, and her nose is swollen and crooked. She wears black flats and speaks with a trembling voice. Her eyes scan the audience, but never settle on me. When she is done, she goes back into the pews and curls up next to the pastor's wife.

I am wearing black pants cut to let my cast hang out and this nice, multi-colored blouse. The nicest stuff I own.

I finger my crutches and hope they provide an excuse. *I can't make my way up there, I'm having trouble walking.* It would take too long, be too big a scene.

My father squeezes my hand.

I close my eyes and focus on the blackness.

Cassie doesn't talk to me after the funeral. She moves through the crowd, walking around and hugging everyone. Which is *not* something Cassie would normally do.

"Can we get out of here?" I ask my dad.

"Are you sure?"

"Yes. Please."

Hey, Chloe. Today was the funeral.

My funeral? Wow. I bet that was weird.

Yeah. Really weird. And I just kept thinking about my mom and wondering what hers was like. Which is messed up, because I don't even really know her, and I know you a million times more. And I should have been thinking about you.

Hey, I get it. You don't want to be thinking about me right now.

Cassie wouldn't even look at me.

It's Cassie, you know? She's going to be like that. She'll get over it.

What the hell did I do?
You remind her of me.
Yeah.

I go back to school on Tuesday. Cassie isn't there.

A random blond girl comes up and tries to hug me. I push her back, maybe a little hard.

Susan in my math class looks up when I sit down, then leans over and whispers, "Oh my god, are you OK?"

I level her with a glare.

How the hell does she think I am?

Ms. Simms, the new guidance counselor, drags me into her office in the afternoon. The place is windowless and stuffy. A red plastic cup, the kind normally filled with beer, sits on her desk, holding a cache of pens.

"It's OK to cry," she tells me. She has dark brown hair and is wearing a blue top. She tries to bore her eyes into mine.

I smile what I hope is an FU smile and say, "No thanks, that's OK."

She stares at me awhile.

I keep smiling. It is fake and plastic and etched onto me.

"You should talk about your loss," she says, drumming her fingers on the peeling faux wood of her desk. "It's healthy."

"Maybe," I say, still smiling. "But I really don't feel like talking to a stranger." I keep that smile frozen on my face.

"Sometimes that can help," she says. "To talk with someone who isn't so close to things."

"Well, thanks for the offer," I tell her, doing my best bouncy-cheerleader Chloe impression. "I think I'll stick to talking to people I actually know for now. Thanks, though."

I make as dramatic an exit from a tiny office as I can while on crutches. Which is to say: I stumble, bang my backpack into the filing cabinet, and eventually hobble out.

After school I go to practice and sit on the bleachers, the

basketballs thudding in my skull, trying to balance my chemistry homework on my outstretched leg.

I go home and watch football with my brothers.

A week ago I had two best friends.

I turn the volume up until even my brother Bill, whose car shakes the whole house when the stereo is on, can't stand it anymore.

Cassie comes back on Wednesday.

"Hi," she says to me while I attempt to cram my backpack into my locker while balancing on one leg.

Her face looks horrible—two black eyes and a swollen nose that looks like it might start bleeding again at any time.

"Um, hi," I say.

"This is so weird," she says. I don't know if she means her talking to me or just being back. At school. Without Chloe.

"Yeah," I say. It's like we have forgotten how to talk to each other. I notice a black scuff mark on the white tile floor and wonder if my crutches have somehow caused it.

She shifts from one foot to the other. "Well, I have class," she says.

"OK," I say.

I didn't get to ask her. About the accident. If she had listened to me.

At lunch, I sit down in my usual spot at her table. She gives me a bit of a look. Like, *What are you doing here?* with her thick dark eyebrows raised.

She says nothing.

And I realize I was *never* going to ask her my question, not in a million years.

We eat in silence.

She is staring at Matt, because of course she would be

staring at Matt. It seems they are in a fight. They'll be all over each other again within a week. That's how it goes with them.

It was the same with Chloe and Glen.

I am suddenly not hungry anymore.

Without saying a word, I rise to one leg, sling both crutches under one arm, pick up my tray, and attempt to balance it while hobbling to the trash.

The tray shakes with every step. Soda spills out.

The noise of the cafeteria rushes into my ears. Then the smells, the processed meat and greasy pizza smells.

My stomach turns over.

"Let me get that."

I look up, eyes narrowed, but it's just Glen, Chloe's ex. I'd seen him at the funeral. He'd looked pale and drawn and sad.

I let him take the tray, and I shift the crutches so that they each support one arm.

Glen has sandy blond hair and a crooked nose. He is built, too, from all the two-a-days. I know exactly what Chloe saw in him. Perky cheerleader, meet gorgeous football player. Fall in love, fight, break up, make up, wash, rinse, repeat.

We don't like him, Cassie and I.

"I am going nucking futs," he says.

"I know," I say. Just to be nice.

"It's messed up," he says. "Half the kids here don't give a shit about me. They figure Chloe and I were broken up, so apparently I didn't care about her anymore. Then there's this group of girls who are all over me, so concerned. All they really want to do is get in my pants."

I snort.

"What's so funny?"

"You kind of sound like a girl right now."

"Shut up," he says, cocking an eyebrow. "It's hard to be this good looking."

I shake my head and hobble off down the hall.

· · ·

"She wasn't even wearing her seat belt," I hear one of them saying. "It would make a good PSA."

I am standing in a bathroom stall, trying to balance on one leg while pulling up my jeans.

"Dumb cheerleader," another says.

"I heard Miss Perfect just pulled out right in front of another car."

"Maybe she was trying to bump Chloe off."

"Shut up," a giggling voice says.

I get my jeans buckled, open the stall door, and stumble out.

"Oh," the blond one says, looking at me. "Sorry."

"Oops," the brunette says.

I lift my crutch and nail the brunette in the knee.

"Owwwww!" she wails.

The blond is at the furthest sink, near the door. I raise my eyebrows at her.

"C'mon, Shelly," she says, grabbing the brunette by the arm and dragging her away. Shelly is hopping on one leg, clutching her knee.

I smile.

Hey, Chloe. Don't listen to them. They're idiots.

I should have been wearing my seat belt.

Why weren't you?

I don't know; I was distracted. I had changed seats, I was checking my phone, remember?

Yeah.

We were just in the parking lot. Mostly.

Yeah.

Would I have lived? If I had been wearing it?

I don't know.

You should ask your dad. I bet he would know.

Sure, yeah.

You won't ask him, will you?
No.

"Did you attack Shelly Porter in the bathroom with your crutches?" Ms. Simms asks forty minutes later. That is how little shame Shelly has.

"No," I say. "She tripped."

"Normally we would suspend a student for something like this." She raises an eyebrow.

"She tripped," I repeat, staring across the desk at her. "I'm sorry; I'm not very good with the crutches yet. It was not intentional."

She smiles at me. "I'm just going to put it down as a misunderstanding," she says.

"OK," I say.

"What the hell?" Cassie asks, running up to my locker. "I heard you attacked Shelly Porter."

"Yeah," I smile slightly.

"That could get you suspended, which could get you kicked off the team!"

"Oh, yeah, I'm really going to miss sitting on the bleachers and watching the team run drills," I say. I turn to glare at her. "What the hell do you care?"

"What do you mean, 'what the hell do I care?'"

"Whatever," I say. "Just leave me alone." I slam the locker closed with my crutch and brush past her, not even bothering to spin the combination lock.

Knowing Cassie, it will drive her nuts and she'll do it for me.

———

CHLOE

Are you OK?

ME

I'm fine.

CHLOE

Well, that's bull. You practically knocked him down.

CASSIE

You could ruin everything.

CHLOE

Chill, Cass. Hopefully he'll decide he doesn't want everyone talking about how he got beat up by a girl. Otherwise, you miss a few games. No big deal. The college scouts won't be looking until junior year.

CASSIE

Colleges look at everything. Getting suspended for shoving a classmate—

CHLOE

If you're an athlete, that's, like, a plus. Yay, she's aggressive. Anyway, that's not what's important here. What the hell is going on?

ME

Nothing. It's fine. He said some stuff. I shoved him.

CHLOE

What did he say?

ME

Nothing important.

CHLOE

You shoved him. It had to be important.

ME

Just drop it, OK?

CASSIE

Remember who you're talking to . . .

CHLOE

You know I'm never going to drop it.

ME

It was about you, OK? And I'm not repeating it, so . . .

CHLOE

Oh.

CASSIE

What?

CHLOE

It's nothing. Just let it go.

CASSIE

What is it?

ME

Just drop it, Cass.

———

I am sitting at practice skimming my history book, my leg propped on the bleacher, when I feel the seat below me sink slightly and look up to see Glen.

"Hi," he says. He is wearing a green hoodie. It matches his eyes.

"Aren't you supposed to be at practice?" I ask.

He shrugs. "I just quit."

"Seriously?"

"Yeah. Coach was giving me a hard time and telling me to run a bunch of laps, and I just thought, *Screw this*. I mean, why the hell am I torturing myself? Life's short. So I walked off."

"That's kind of awesome and kind of stupid."

He grins. "Yeah." He has a nice smile. His whole face kind of ripples upward.

I remind myself why we do not like him, Cassie and I.

"I heard you beat up Shelly Porter," he says.

"So it's hit the rumor mill," I say. "Awesome. Maybe they'll all leave me alone now."

"Whatever she did, she had it coming." He smiles, dimples caving in.

I smile, in spite of myself.

The basketballs thud loudly in the background. Coach blows her whistle. Silence, then they start up again.

"Why haven't you quit?" he asks. He glances down at my leg. "The season's shot."

I shrug. "I don't know. I want to make sure I still have a spot next year."

"If you're good, they'll forgive you," he says. "If not, well, screw it."

I smile and then stop myself.

"Did you start the rumor about her?" I ask. I don't want to say her name.

"The one that we had sex?"

"Yeah."

"I guess. I mean, not intentionally. Don't girls tell their friends when they, you know? I mean, I guess I just need better friends."

I guess girls don't tell each other, I think.

"She was into that promise ring stuff with Cassie. Saving herself or whatever," I say.

He shrugs. "Yeah, I go to church every week and I'm an atheist. Just because she put on the ring to fit in and whatever . . ."

"Right," I say.

"She was on the pill," he says.

I remember, then. Chloe shoving her hand in her purse on the way to school that morning. Swallowing something the size of a Tic Tac and saying something about having a headache.

"Can you give me a ride home?" I ask.

"Don't you have another hour of practice?"

"Let's just get out of here."

He sticks his hand in his pocket, pulls out a ring of keys, and jingles them in my face. Smiles again. His face creases in all the right places.

. . .

Hey, Chloe. So you weren't a virgin?

I guess not.

Why didn't you tell me? I mean, Cassie I get. But me? I don't judge. Why didn't you tell me?

You didn't like Glen. Neither of you.

I was always nice about him.

I could tell, though.

Well, I'm sorry.

It's OK. We broke up, in the end.

I wish I would have known.

Why?

I wish I knew you better.

You knew me, Ky. You knew me so well you know everything I'd say.

Maybe. Maybe not.

Don't be like that. You know I loved you. You were my best friend.

I know.

Without basketball, Glen starts giving me a ride home every day. We stop off at the bakery or the bowling alley to have a snack, then watch a game or two at my house until he has to go home. My brothers eye him up and down. I have two who live at home, one who lives here whenever his girlfriend kicks him out (which is a lot of the time), and one who's off at sleepaway college and comes home every other weekend.

"He was Chloe's . . . friend," I tell them after Glen leaves the first day. "We're keeping each other company."

"You should be at basketball," Joe says, twisting the tab on his soda.

"Sitting on the bleachers trying to keep my leg comfortable? What's the point?"

"Teamwork and all that."

"Sounds super fun. I'm not doing that anymore. Get over it."

"Are you doing OK?"

"Shove it."

They warm up to Glen, though. He doesn't swipe the remote or change the channels. He is always willing to go grab someone a soda or a beer.

When my brothers aren't around, we mute the game sometimes.

"We were supposed to get back together," he says during halftime one day.

"Yeah?" I take my eyes off the TV.

Glen is staring down at the zipper on his sweatshirt, working it between his fingers. "We always got back together, didn't we?"

"Yeah, you always did. No matter what we tried to tell her . . . she loved you."

He chuckles. We are splitting a beer from the fridge. A dribble of foam leaks out his nose and he laughs.

"You're disgusting," I tell him.

He laughs harder.

"She ever tell you what she did for prom?" he asks. "We didn't have any money for a nice car or a room or anything, but she got these stickers off the internet and did up my car to make it look like a Mercedes. A really poor excuse for a Mercedes, but it was funny. And then she found this spot, out in the woods. She draped all this fabric so it was like a tent, a really cool, I don't know, Indian one. From India, Indian. The fabric would blow around in the breeze and it was nice. And she had an air mattress with nice sheets and candles and everything."

Why the hell didn't she tell me any of this stuff? Just "Going to prom with Glen." "Do you like this dress?" "What should I do with my hair?"

The pricy updo she'd had done was messed up the next day. I just assumed she'd slept on it wrong.

"That sounds like Chloe," I say. I reach for the beer and take a sip. We have to finish it before anyone gets home.

"The stupid stickers wouldn't come off, though. I got pissed and bitched at her the next day and she was crying and stormed off and we were broken up for a week. I got most of them off, but you can still see bits and pieces . . ."

We always assumed Glen had wanted prom to be extra special, Chloe said no, and he dumped her.

"She never told us why you guys would break up," I say. "Was it always stupid stuff like that?"

"Sometimes," he says, taking the beer back and looking away. "Sometimes I would look at another girl or one would come up to me and flirt or whatever. I never slept with them, but . . ." He shrugged. "I may have danced with them or let one of them kiss me when I was drunk. I didn't cheat, though. I would never cheat on her.

"It's weird," he continues, "because nobody cares that my ex-girlfriend died. I mean, my parents care a little bit. They ask about it; they blame it for whatever stupid thing I do. But nobody really gets it. It's as if they all think, *You were broken up, what do you care?*"

"It's not like you can't be in love with someone and break up with them."

"Exactly." He drains the remains of the beer.

"I could do with less people caring," I tell him.

"Shelly Porter didn't scare them off?" He crushes the empty can against his head.

"Not really. Not enough of them. Not the guidance counselor, not my family. They're all constantly asking if I'm OK. It's really annoying. I think they want the answer to be no, which makes me want to just punch one of them. If the answer is yes, they don't believe me. If it's no, what the hell are they going to do with it? Say, 'It gets better?' That will really make me want to punch them."

Glen smiles. "For the record, I am so not OK."

"Yeah, I figured. You were drunk at school yesterday."

"You noticed?" He looks at me with raised eyebrows.

I smile. "Everyone noticed. People talk."

"Screw 'em."

"Screw 'em," I concur.

"You know you're not OK," he says.

"Oh, I know."

He grins and rises to dispose of the beer. "I don't think it gets better," he says.

I relax into the couch.

———

CHLOE
Well, we're through.
CASSIE
Who?
CHLOE
Me and Glen. He broke up with me.
ME
You'll get back together.
CHLOE
I don't think so. Not this time.
ME
You always get back together.
CASSIE
Against our collective better judgment.
CHLOE
I screwed it up. I screwed it all up.
ME
What did you do?
CASSIE

Trust me, you didn't screw it up. You just made the best decision of your life. You are so much better off without him.

CHLOE

Screw you!

ME

Not the time, Cass.

CASSIE

Just get over him already. He sucks. There are better fish in the sea. Matt's drummer—

CHLOE

Shut the hell up!

CASSIE

OK, sorry. Chlo, I'm sorry. What happened?

CHLOE

Nothing, I just. I messed it up.

ME

What did you do? It can't be worse than all the stuff he did.

CHLOE

I was at a party and this guy on his team started flirting with me . . .

CASSIE

Chlo, he flirts with other girls all the time. I can't count the number of times I've seen him over with some little slut—

ME

Little slut, really? Way to advance the cause.

CASSIE

I'm trying to make her feel better.

CHLOE

I think I just . . . I have to get home. I'll talk to you guys tomorrow.

———

"What are you doing with Glen?" Cassie asks me in October. She sits down across from me at lunch, at our usual spot.

The spot she has only sporadically frequented the last six weeks.

"What do you mean?" I roll a fry through my mouth with my tongue, sucking in the salty goodness.

Cassie wrinkles up her fully healed nose. "I mean, you're hanging out all the time," she says. She stabs at her salad.

And you've hardly said two words to me. Sorry I've moved on.

"We watch sports," I say finally. I take a sip of Mountain Dew.

"He was Chloe's boyfriend," she says.

"Yeah, I know."

"You can't hook up with him. It's really, *really* wrong."

I push back my lunch tray and stand as best I can. "Yeah, no duh," I say. "We're friends. We talk about Chloe. Since I clearly don't have anyone else to talk to."

"Excuse me," she says, also rising. "I am having a really hard time with all of this. I am running two clubs this semester, I work twenty-five hours a week, I'm taking an AP class, and I have to keep my 4.0."

"I'm sorry that being a friend doesn't fit into your schedule," I say, my fist clenching.

"Oh please," she says. "I'm in the same place you are. I'm trying to deal with the fact that my best friend is dead. So sorry I'm not around to ask how you're feeling and get shoved away. I have my own broken heart to try to heal."

"Like you even have a heart," I say.

She ignores me. "And I've seen the way Glen looks at you. I already lost one friend to that jerk."

"Get over it," I tell her. "You didn't lose Chloe because of Glen. You lost Chloe because you drove your car in front of an SUV."

I think I see a tear graze her cheek before she whips around and marches out of the cafeteria.

I stand there, balanced on one leg, trembling, watching

the place where the doors closed shut behind her. The doors stop swinging, and I keep trembling.

Then, because I have nothing better to do, I drop back down to my bench. And because I kind of hate her, I reach over and take possession of her fries.

"So how's it going?" Ms. Simms asks. I have been summoned out of history class and sit slouched across the desk from her, arms crossed.

"Fine."

She looks down and ruffles some papers on her desk.

"I heard you had a fight with Cassie," she says, looking back up.

Apparently she has spies.

"And . . ."

"It can be hard, after a loss . . ."

"Your point?"

"Sometimes it can help to talk about it. Maybe with an old friend, or maybe with someone who isn't so close to the situation."

"Someone like you?"

"It can help," she says.

"That's super," I say. I try kicking at her desk with my cast, but it just sends a shiver of pain up my leg.

"Look, Kyra, do you have anyone to talk to?" she asks. She clasps her hands together and rests her chin in them. Looks straight at me. "I don't care who. Do you have someone?"

"Yeah, I have someone."

"Is it helping?" She drums her fingers on her lower lip.

I relax my leg. "Yeah, I think so."

"Is it getting any easier?"

"I don't know," I tell her, letting my arms drift to my sides. "Is it supposed to?"

She tilts her head back and gazes up at the florescent

lighting. "I honestly don't know," she says. She looks back at me. "I'm sorry." She sighs. "I haven't done this in fifteen years. I was prepared to help kids pick a college, maybe deal with an eating disorder . . ."

"You're doing fine," I tell her. "Really. It's better if you don't think you have all the answers. You'll be wrong a lot less."

She tilts back her head and laughs.

———

CASSIE
You guys would. Not. Believe. The day I've had.
CHLOE
What happened?
CASSIE
Well, first of all, they messed up my schedule. So they give me the printout and it has two classes I've already taken, regular English, some cooking elective that I'm half tempted to cry "sexism" on and—
NEW GIRL
Um, excuse me, hi. I'm new here and—
CHLOE
Oh, hi! I'm Chloe. Where are you from? How do you like it? This school's kind of small. Which makes it kind of great when new people show up, because, you know, something different. But it can take some getting used to. How big was your old school? Cassie, Kyra, you guys going to say hi at any point?
ME
Maybe if you ever shut-up. Hi.
CASSIE
What's up?
NEW GIRL

Um, I was just wondering if I could maybe get a ride home.
I'm not far . . .
CASSIE
Close enough to walk?
ME
Geez, Cassie, way to be a bitch.
CASSIE
I'm just trying to find out how far. I'm on a tight schedule here.
CHLOE
Oh, whatever. Ignore her. She's practicing for when she grows
up and has one of those busy corporate lawyer lives. We can
totally give you a ride. Here, take my seat.
NEW GIRL
That's OK.
CHLOE
Common courtesy. New girl gets shotgun. When you ride
with us tomorrow, we can boot you to the back with Kyra.
ME
We were supposed to rotate shotgun.
CHLOE
Maybe when you pass your road test.
What was your name again?
NEW GIRL
Lacey.
CHLOE
Welcome. This place kind of sucks, but we're here, so . . .
CASSIE
Sorry, she's insufferable sometimes.
ME
She's insufferable? Really?
CASSIE
I am extremely driven and have high standards. There's a
difference.
ME

Well, Miss Extremely Driven, can you please just *drive* and get us the hell out of here?

CASSIE

We're going, we're going.

CHLOE

Ooh, someone's texting me.

CASSIE

It better not be Glen.

CHLOE

Shut the F up, would you? Anyway, it's not him.

ME

C'mon, Chlo, you have to admit he treated you like crap.

CHLOE

Just shut up about Glen already, would you?

CASSIE

Why? You never shut up about him.

CHLOE

Don't make me beg.

CASSIE

Sorry. We just love you and want you to be with someone who deserves you.

ME

Someone like Matt?

CASSIE

Shut up. What's wrong with Matt?

CHLOE

Ask us again tomorrow when you stop speaking because, I don't know, you say something that he takes the wrong way or he doesn't really care enough about such-and-such.

CASSIE

Whatever. He loves me.

ME

Can you turn already?

CASSIE

I'm checking for cars.

CHLOE

Maybe that's why you never passed your road test, Ky.

ME

On second thought, you *are* insuf—

———

My cast comes off in November and Glen suggests we cele-
brate. We drive two towns over to a bowling alley that doesn't
card, and we play two games. Glen laughs every time I walk
up to the lane, since I am wobbly on my new leg. It's thinner
than my good leg; all the muscle shriveled. Thank god I'm not
doing basketball this fall—my stats would tank.

"You walk like a penguin," he says.

I give him the finger and drive the ball down the lane.
Gutter ball.

"Ouch," he says.

By the end of the second game, the pitcher he ordered is
drained and I am crushing him. I grow steadier as he begins
to sway.

"So this is the secret to winning?" I ask. "Get you drunk?"

"The secret to cheating, maybe."

"I didn't force you to drink."

"You didn't help me finish off the pitcher." Outside of a
few sips, I really haven't. My dad doesn't work this far out of
town, but he is friendly with the neighboring cops. If
anything goes down, I want to be able to say I was just there
to bowl.

"God forbid good beer goes to waste."

"Hey, I paid fifteen dollars for this," he says, lip puffing
out in a pout.

"It tastes like warm piss. You overpaid."

He laughs.

"I may have added a little something," he says.

"Warm piss?"

He laughs again.

We try our hand at pool, but I crush him. At one point he is half lying across the green felt table while I take shots around him (and occasionally at his stomach).

"Everybody hates me," he says.

Great. The sad drunk. "I don't hate you," I tell him.

"Not yet."

"Chloe loved you."

"No she didn't." He flops over onto his back and stares up at the tiles on the drop ceiling.

"She wanted to get back together with you. She told us. She thought she had screwed everything up. She definitely still loved you."

"If she had loved me, she never would have slept with him."

I freeze, cue dangling from my hand. "What do you mean?"

"She cheated on me," he says. He puts his hands over his eyes. "We had a fight, I was looking funny at another girl or something; she decided to even the score, found some guy, and started crawling all over him."

"But they didn't—"

"Oh, no, they did. Ben walked in on them."

Hey, Chloe, did I even know you at all?

No, I guess not.

"She was all apologies the next day. Said she hated herself for it or whatever. Was crying and kept trying to hug me . . . I wanted to punch her."

My fist clenches around the cue.

"I didn't," he adds quickly. "I tried to go punch him, well, I guess I did go punch him. But he kicked my ass. I was still hungover and he just . . . so, yeah, I pretty much suck on every level."

"I'm sorry," I say. I let the cue drop to the ground and listen to its clatter.

"I miss her," he says. "I should have told her I still loved her. I should have just let it go. I should have given her a ride that day. I just keep thinking . . . she died thinking that I . . . that I hated her. She died thinking that."

I start to tell him she didn't, but what the hell do I know?

Finally, I just say, "We should leave."

The night air is crisp and smells of burning leaves.

When we get to the car, he fumbles with his keys and I gently pry them away, my fingers brushing his.

"You don't have a license," he mumbles.

"You're drunk," I say.

I drive slowly. Not so slow as to attract police attention, but slow. I come to a complete stop at every intersection, even the ones without stop signs.

We drive through cornfields down deserted two-lane highways, the stars twinkling above. I wonder how it is that I have ended up here.

"I loved her," Glen sobs in the passenger seat.

I make a mental note to never let him get more than one beer in him again. This was not the carefree night of celebration I had in mind.

"I loved her," he says again.

"I know," I tell him.

When we get to his house, the lights are out. His parents are old, probably asleep already. I find the house key and help him out of the passenger seat. He practically throws his arms around me while I pull him up the porch steps and through the front door. Down the hall to his room, the only bedroom on the first floor, thank god. I wonder how many times he has done this before. Has Chloe helped to drag him in?

Of course she has. It was in her nature.

But what the hell do I really know of her nature anymore?

I lay him down in his bed, peel off his shoes.

"I need to go," I say, leaning over him. "Are you going to choke to death on your own vomit or anything?"

He reaches his arms up and pulls me toward him. Presses his tongue into my mouth. His lips are soft and smooth, his tongue tart and nimble.

I shove up, break out of his mouth, out of his arms.

"I love you," he says.

"You're drunk," I say, shifting my weight to my bad leg.

"You would never cheat on me," he says.

I reach my hand out and brush his face. "She loved you," I tell him. "She told me. Just a day or two before she died. She told me, 'I'm still in love with Glen. I need to fix things.' That's what she said."

"She's dead."

"I know."

"I love you."

"No you don't, Glen." I stop stroking his face.

"You don't love me," he says. His eyes are pooled with sorrow.

"I'm sorry," I say. I look away. "I'm possibly the reason the girl you do love is dead."

He doesn't hear me. "No one loves me," he says. He rolls over onto his face.

Maybe you should try cleaning yourself up and stop feeling sorry for yourself, I think. *Maybe you should just get over it already.*

I don't say it.

"You love Chloe," I say. "You love Chloe. You just need time. You still love Chloe."

His words are muffled in the pillow.

I try touching his shoulder, but he shrugs it back.

How the hell did I get here?

Hey, Chloe, your skeezy ex just tried to kiss me.

I know. That's like, crazy, right?

I don't know why you ever put up with him.

He could be sweet. He loved me. He wanted to be better. I thought I could save him.

You can't save everyone.

I know. But you know, I screwed up too.

Yeah, but you were a good person.

So is he. Sometimes.

You were always good. Even when you did things . . . It doesn't really matter, you know? I still love you.

I know.

I shouldn't have told Cassie to speed up.

She didn't listen to you. You know she never does.

I know, that's what I keep telling myself.

I know.

I miss you.

I know.

I walk home. Two miles. Good practice for next season.

The air is cold and crisp; leaves crunch beneath my feet. I never liked the cold, but the air, thin and sharp against my nostrils, feels cleansing somehow. *Like a breath of fresh air*, the cliché would go. With every few steps, I take a deep breath, let it rest in my lungs.

My leg is aching by the time I get home. But my sinuses feel better than they have in months.

There is a basketball lying beside the driveway and a pair of baseball bats propped up against the garage, same as always. The paint on the back door is peeling, and I have to jiggle my key to get in.

Inside, dishes pile high in the sink and every chair has one or more coats draped over it. I practically trip over the pile of large, smelly, muddy shoes amassed in front of me on my way to dumping my coat on the top of a heap.

Once upon a time, I think we had a coat rack.

But I like it like this.

"You were out late," my father says when I pass through the living room. He's spun in the recliner to look me up and down. He is the only one home; the boys must all be out with friends.

"Sorry," I say. "I thought you were working."

"Slow night," he says. "They let me go. I'm glad you're actually getting out of the house. But next time you stay out that late . . ." He wags a finger at me and raises his eyebrows.

"I know," I say.

"Have fun?" he asks.

"Not really."

"Sorry to hear that."

I shrug and start to head upstairs.

Then I stop on the second stair and turn back. "Hey, I have a question," I say.

"Shoot."

"If Chloe—" I say. "If she had been wearing her seat belt . . ."

He is quiet for a moment, his eyes locked on mine. Then he shrugs. "I don't know," he says.

I nod.

"I want to say this is why you always wear your goddamn seat belt, but I know the prosecutor has some expert witness is who going to say that it wouldn't have mattered."

"Really?"

"Well, I mean, you can pretty much find an expert to fit any theory, but yeah, he says the way the car was hit, she would have snapped back and hit the glass either way. It was one of those subcompact things. They don't hold up to side impacts very well."

"Thanks," I say.

"Sure," he says.

I get partway up the third step, then stop.

I go back and wrap my arms around my father's balding head.

He reaches up and rubs my back, and I let him.

Later that night, lying in bed, I notice that my leg feels funny, like the halo of the cast is still there.

I think about how my leg can heal up perfect, but it still won't be the same.

Then I exhale and let that thought drift up into the nether region.

I let it drift up to her, and then I let it go.

3

INTERIOR DIALOG

The thing Amanda didn't expect was how much she would miss being able to drive. How difficult the simplest things could be when that privilege was taken away.

Like, months ago, breaking the silence with Sam, her husband, to say, "I need you to drive me to the lawyer's." He looked up at her, the glare of his computer screen reflecting off his wire rims, and said nothing. After a moment, his face drew together and he nodded slightly. A few minutes later they headed out to the car, the early autumn leaves crunching beneath their feet.

It was worse still having to venture to the basement to ask Matt, her seventeen-year-old son: "Will you drive me to the grocery store?"

He was flipping through a magazine and looked up with narrowed eyes. He scanned her up and down, then let out a sigh so loud it sounded as though he were clearing his throat.

"I guess," he said. "Do you need me to wait in the car for you? Or just pick you up in an hour?"

Her mouth fluttered a few times. "You can just pick me up later," she finally whispered.

She stared at him as he drove, his gaze fixed firmly on the

road. She thought about how, as a baby, he smiled every time he saw her face. How he had woken her up, every two hours like clockwork, until he was six months old. How, in the end, she didn't really mind, because the moment she came up to his crib, the screaming would stop and a great toothless grin would erupt across his face. He would stare into her eyes then, like she was the whole world.

She never expected Matt to hate her. She never expected to lose *him*.

Jade, her niece, who Amanda had cared for in her childhood, who'd always come over whenever she'd had a fight with her mom, was no longer speaking to her. Jade, whose first steps she had witnessed (but been careful not to mention to Janice); Jade, the streak of wild hair running through her backyard; Jade, who always spoke her mind, consequences be damned; Jade was no longer showing up at their house midnights after fights with her mother. No longer sending texts, no longer calling for rides. Not coming near her. Just gone.

The only one who was speaking to her was Jenna. Her fourteen-year-old daughter was supposed to hate her mother for no good reason, and now had every good reason. She had been riding in the car with Amanda when the accident happened, when that girl *died*, and was probably traumatized by it all, though it didn't show. Jenna, the baby of the family, the one she should protect.

But Jenna kept smiling at her. Fiddling with her red hair and seeking out Amanda to ask about her day, or asking if she wanted to go to the park, to watch a TV show, to see something cool on the internet.

When Jenna was a baby, there had been none of the joy of waking with her. Amanda had a three-year-old to chase all day. Jenna's nighttime waking was an inconvenience. And Jenna never smiled when she entered. Jenna just kept screaming and screaming, no matter what she tried.

But it was Matt—her angel baby—who hated her now.

She couldn't blame him, she really couldn't. He had known Chloe. He was in love with Chloe's best friend. Of course he would hate her. She deserved it.

"You could have killed Jenna," Sam had said to her that day when he came to pay her bail, the way she knew he would. He didn't say anything else, didn't bury the knife.

And she said nothing, because what could she say? They had booked her on a DUI (a mistake with their equipment, she was sure). But they'd told her, at the station. The charge was now vehicular manslaughter.

Chloe had died.

Today, she calls Renata for a ride: "I just really need to get out of the house."

Sitting in Renata's cozy living room, on her worn green microfiber sofa, staring at Renata's twinkling Christmas lights, Amanda says, "Sam's texting another woman."

Renata leans in, eyebrows hopping up. "He's stepping out?"

"No . . . I don't . . . I don't think so. They're just having coffee. As friends. He has a lot . . . to deal with. With me."

"And he should be talking to *you*, not some other woman."

"He doesn't," Amanda says. He never has, not when his problems were with her. She was the same way. When Matt was an infant, she'd come down with the flu on the same night as some important elbow-rubbing thing at Sam's work. Sam had gone, but that was (somewhat) understandable. What she couldn't understand, much less forgive, was that he'd then stayed out half the night, while she sat at home, fever blazing, rocking a screaming baby and sobbing.

By the time he came home, she was too tired to fight. And the next morning, it hardly seemed worth it, not when she needed him to take care of Matt so she could (finally) rest.

She's nursed it for years, but it always seemed petty to bring it up after so much time had passed.

"Neither of us talk," she tells Renata.

"Yeah, well, you need to," Renata insists. "Y'all need to have this out. Go home, pack a bag, confront him, lay it all out, and then see if you still want to be there. If not, I'll be waiting in your driveway with the car running."

"It's fine," Amanda says. "I trust him." *I can't leave him,* she thinks. *I can't be alone.*

"Bullshit," Renata says. "Maybe it is all innocent, but you know things aren't fine."

Things were fine until they weren't. That was how it always was with them. And then, a day or a week or a month later, they were fine again. Without doing anything, really. Just waking up, eating breakfast, and pretending nothing had happened.

After a glass of wine, Renata drives her home, carefully navigating the slushy roads. "I'll be waiting," Renata says, letting her out in front of the house.

"Not tonight," Amanda tells her.

"Sweetie, you have to do it. Yank the damn Band-Aid off." Renata rests a hand on her arm. "There's never going to be a good time. You wouldn't have told me if you didn't want me to push you."

"I screwed up," she says. "I ruined everything."

"Girl, it takes two," Renata tells her. "He either wants to save the marriage or he doesn't. If he wants to, then you just need to nudge him along. If not . . ."

"Better to know now," she hears herself whisper as she steps onto the slippery blanket of snow covering her lawn.

Amanda goes inside. She can hear Sam in his office, the clicking of his keyboard whirling away. The door is, of course, closed. To better avoid her.

The children are behind closed doors as well. Matt's music is blasting up from the basement, and light pours down the stairway that leads up to Jenna's attic room.

They didn't used to be like this. Before, they would all be gathered here, in the open-concept living area, snacking on chips, flipping through channels on the TV, arguing and joking amongst themselves.

She thinks about the cacophony she is used to hearing:

"Mom, tell him to share the remote."

"I was here first."

"No, you weren't. I was watching *Sailor Moon*, then a commercial came on and you changed it over to whatever the hell this is."

"It's *Man vs. Food*, and I'm talking about the planet. I was here first on the planet."

"You suck. That's so not fair."

"Life's not fair. The sooner you stop struggling and trying to make things fair, and accept the way they are, the happier you'll be. You're welcome, by the way, for the wisdom."

And then, Sam, at the dining room table on his laptop, completely oblivious to the children's bickering, as usual: "Honey, can you look this over? I'm onto the Peloponnesian War. It doesn't quite sound right . . ."

Except when she and Sam were fighting. Not *fighting*. They didn't fight. They just . . . stewed. The kids covered the silence in bickering.

"What's your favorite breakfast food?"

"I don't know, pancakes?"

"That's a horrible choice. Full of carbs."

"You didn't ask what the *best* breakfast food was, just what my favorite was."

"Your favorite should take into account more than just taste."

"Oh my god! I don't care if it's unhealthy. I like pancakes. You ate pancakes last week!"

"Yeah, well, that was before I knew about carbs."

She thinks about how the kids have been holed away since the accident, lost in their own little cones of silence. Matt is angry, so he says nothing. Jenna just pretends everything is fine. *They learned it from us,* she thinks.

After he picked her up that night, she could only guess at what Sam was thinking. She had always thought it a mercy, the way they bit their tongues, avoided yelling, avoided saying anything that could wound.

Now it seems the ultimate form of cruelty. To leave her here, twisting, for months, playing it over and over again in her head, imagining what he is thinking, what he is wishing he could say.

He says normal things to her: "Need a ride?" And, "I have that meeting at three." And, "We're out of milk."

He even asks what she wants for breakfast.

But what he doesn't do is look her in the eyes. He doesn't reach for her in the middle of the night, doesn't kiss her on the way out the door.

Doesn't say a word about the thing neither of them can stop thinking about.

The closest he has come to even mentioning the accident is to complain about his sister Janice, who is footing the bill for Amanda's lawyer. At Thanksgiving, Janice made a point of mentioning how happy she was to help out. They shouldn't worry about the cost at all, she said, arm on Amanda's shoulder. She didn't understand people who don't help out their family when needed, she said. She had the money, she repeated, so she might as well use it now, for this.

"Well that was fun," Sam said after dinner. "I knew she would do it, too. There are no strings with my sister . . . except the need for her to continually use it to stroke her own ego."

Amanda almost said something. They could bond over it, how difficult Janice was. How Janice's own daughter hadn't shown for Thanksgiving dinner. But then Amanda realized that *she* might actually be the reason Jade avoided the gathering. Aunt Amanda, the killer.

And she remembered that the fancy lawyer may be her salvation. That Janice was showing her support in the only way she knew, which was with money.

And Sam, Sam had been showing how he felt the only way he knew, which was with silence. And she would not let him pretend otherwise.

So she ignored him and put the leftovers in the fridge.

She used to think the lawyer could save them. That the judge would find her not guilty, that Sam would believe him, that they would all collectively pretend these last months hadn't happened.

Because it is possible that she is not a horrible, irresponsible murderer.

The other driver, Cassie, pulled out in front of her. She'd only had her license a week. Probably hadn't looked. Amanda certainly hadn't seen her, not until it was too late.

She feels a pain in her gut, thinking about Cassie like this. She knows Cassie, she loves Cassie. Matt's first serious girlfriend. Intense, driven, a powder keg of pressure. If she didn't implode, she'd likely be running the world one day.

She thinks about the evenings Cassie would come over. After school, after whatever planning committee or honor society she was on, and after work. Sometimes she would disappear into the basement with Matt, but other times she would draw him upstairs. They would sit in the living room, TV on or listening to music (kicking Jenna out if she was already there). Cassie would spread her books across the coffee table.

"Stop!" she would yell at Matt when he inevitably did something, tickling her ribs, stealing her pencil.

"Studies have shown homework has no educational value," he would say.

"I'm not doing it to get an education," she would say back, eyes rolling, lips pursed in a barely repressed smile. "I need to get a full ride to a top-shelf college so I can actually *get* that education."

"Or, you need a library card and a passport."

"Your life is way too easy."

"Mom," she would hear Matt call while she sat at the kitchen table trying not to eavesdrop, "is my life too easy?"

"Oh, undoubtedly," she would say back, with just a glance up at Cassie.

"See, even your mom agrees with me."

"Whatever."

She ventured, one day, to say, "Look, Cassie, it's all going to be OK, you know? You'll get there, I promise. You can relax a little bit."

"My parents relaxed. They ended up knocked up and barely able to keep a running car."

"I'm sorry," Amanda said, drumming her fingers on her lower lip and thinking about how much harder it was to win a race when you started after everyone else. "Still, you're not your parents. You are absolutely going places. I guarantee it."

Cassie shrugged. "Can't take the eyes off the prize," she said.

She had wanted to ask if Cassie was sure that "prize" was really what she wanted, but didn't. Instead she just said, "Take care of yourself."

She thinks that maybe it was no one's fault, just an accident.

Then there was Chloe, the girl who died, who hadn't been wearing her seat belt. Her lawyer said it didn't matter, but Amanda couldn't let it go. If Chloe had just worn her seat belt
. . .

And it was just two drinks at lunch. So little alcohol that it never even crossed her mind that she might be impaired. She certainly hadn't felt impaired.

One stupid mistake. She didn't know, she didn't realize. She'd done a million stupid things in high school, drag raced with the boys, went out drinking with the girls, BSed essay questions because she hadn't read the book.

But she (narrowly) avoided being hit by a truck as she flew through the flashing red. Her parents didn't smell the alcohol on her breath. She got an A on the test.

Bad things didn't happen to her.

Until now.

She thinks about how much she misses the way things used to be.

She has been waiting, holding her breath, for months now.

She thinks about the texts she saw on Sam's phone, from someone named Susanna:

You up?

U know me, up before the sun. What R U doing up?

Cant sleep. Saw Amanda drinking wine at 2 AM. Again.

Not good

No - I don't get it . . . Never thought there was a problem, but who knows

Sorry . . . Coffee?

Yes! Usual spot?

C U soon

She thinks about how the alcohol isn't a problem, never has been. A drink here or there, sure. Everyone did it. A few drinks were supposed to be good for your heart. She thinks about how she never would have thought two watered-down margaritas at Joe's, celebrating the sale of the old McCormick place for just under a half a million dollars (in a down market!), would have put her over the legal limit. They had changed the law at some point; under the old law, she wouldn't have been considered under the influence. How bizarre is that? A piece of paper, a change in a decimal, and all of a sudden her life is torn asunder.

It's ironic, she thinks. She didn't really drink much before the accident, but now she drinks wine most nights. *A self-fulfilling prophecy.* But it is more than that. She drinks at night now because she is sad and alone. Without a driver's license, she can't work, not that anyone would hire her anyway. She sits alone and watches daytime TV and has the same arguments in her head, over and over again. Arguments with lawyers, with the cops, with a theoretical judge, with the kids, with Sam. Then the kids get home, and Matt scatters. Sometimes Jenna hangs out, but all she can think about is how wrong it is that Jenna is trying to cheer her up. When Jenna could have died. Her own mother could have killed her.

She wonders how deep Jenna has buried her anger. What it will look like, one day, when it finally comes to the surface.

And then Sam gets home and they exchange bland conversation, and it is painful, because it is not the way they normally talk. He grabs some food and scurries into his office, coming out only when he is ready to go to bed, and then she sits alone in the kitchen, waiting for the sound of his snoring, before stealthily slipping in beside him.

So of course she has a glass of wine while she is waiting. She also cries silently, brow contorting in the dark, and sometimes she even runs outside into the snow, not properly dressed, and sobs loudly, chest heaving, throat burning, until the tears crystallize and freeze onto her cheeks.

She thinks about how things really can't go on like this. She thinks about how she is tired of waiting for things to get better.

She thinks about the other pair of texts, the ones she didn't mention to Renata.

U think you will leave her?

Don't know

Shaking, she goes to their bedroom, where she awakes alone every morning and feels blindly for the warm spot where he had been. She opens the closet doors and reaches up high for the suitcase. It threatens to fall on her head, but she manages to steady it. It's leopard print, a gift from her aunt half a dozen years ago. The last time she used it was their summer trip to Niagara—the nice version of Niagara, the one on the Canadian side of the border.

Staring down at the crashing water, Sam had pulled her away from the railing and kissed her. One of the kids—probably Matt—had muttered, "Get a room," and they had smiled knowingly at each other.

She figures they won't go on a trip this summer. Assuming everything goes all right in court—and she has to assume that, she can't think about the other possibility—they won't want to spend any money, not when they could have been using it to pay for a lawyer (never mind that their entire vacation fund would buy about an hour with the lawyer). There will be too much guilt from Janice if they go off and spend a dime.

But they could maybe do something small. A weekend away, a staycation. The acquittal would send a message, to both of them. They could start pretending again. *Act as if.* Act as if everything is OK, and it will be OK.

As she thinks this, she is opening drawers, removing carefully folded jeans, t-shirts, socks, underwear, two bras, and wedging them into the suitcase. She grabs two button-down shirts and a nice pair of pants from the closet, in case she needs to meet with her lawyer.

She has to push on the top to get the zipper closed. She realizes that she hasn't packed any books, anything to keep her occupied during the long days of waiting.

She tells herself that she won't be needing any of it. That she will be unpacking in an hour, sending Renata away.

But she needs this. She needs this suitcase, this prop. So she can walk away if she needs to. So he knows that this is it. That it is time to make a decision. Time to forgive her.

She walks to the office and stands staring at his closed door, trying to think of what to say.

It was an accident, she hears herself saying. *I would never—*

It was not an accident! You were drunk. You could have killed Jenna! You did kill that other girl!

It was an accident. What about the time you were high and Matt fell down the stairs? Yeah, it could have happened when you were sober, but it didn't. He could have snapped his neck.

She thinks of that night. She went out with friends and Sam stayed home with Matt. This was before she had a cell phone, so he called the restaurant and a waiter came up and whispered, "We have a phone call for you. It sounds serious."

She could tell from Sam's voice that he was crying. Hyperventilating. "He just fell," he'd said. "I just blinked and he just fell."

"What?" Her breath caught in the back of her throat.

"The basement. The stairs. I forgot to close the door."

Tears sprung to her eyes. "Is he moving? Is he breathing? Is he OK?"

"He—he—he was crying a lot. Screaming. He won't let me put him down."

She let out her breath. She noticed, suddenly, another sound in the background. Matt's tiny sobs. Why hadn't she heard them before?

"Is anything broken?"

"I don't think so."

"You need to take him to the hospital. He could have a concussion. I'll meet you there."

"Um—" he said. "I can't. I can't drive. And I shouldn't be there at the hospital."

"What do you mean?" Her voice grew cold.

"I . . . I just . . . I was worried about my deadline and Matt was making a lot of noise and I just wanted to calm down a bit. Take the edge off. It was just half a joint . . ."

She was not the type to get angry and yell. That was not

who they were. She opened her mouth but no words came out.

"I am so sorry," he said. "I know I fucked up. I am so sorry." He was crying again.

"OK," she said, voice drained of emotion. "I'm going to come pick up Matt. I'll take him to the hospital."

"Thank you," he said. "I'm sorry."

Matt didn't die, she hears Sam saying now. *And I never got high again. I still see you drinking.*

Only because you won't talk to me and I'm miserable! If that's the only problem, I'll throw it all out tonight and never drink again.

That won't bring that girl back to life. That won't make things any better for her parents. All alone in the world.

I wish to God every day that I could undo what I did.

You can't.

It's not fair. When Matt fell down the stairs, I forgave you. He was two years old and you were supposed to keep the goddamn basement door shut and you got high and stupid and my poor baby fell down fourteen steps and banged his head and bruised his arms and he was crying so hard! And I had to go to the hospital all by myself so that CPS wouldn't get involved and declare you an unfit father and me unfit for being stupid enough to trust you with our kid. And I held him and I rocked him for hours and he finally fell asleep in my arms. But I had to wake him up, to keep waking him up, to make him cry over and over again, because the doctor said he might have a concussion and the internet said if he slept he could die. He could have died! Why, why did I forgive you? Why can't you forgive me?

Did you though? Did you? When Matt started getting those migraines, I know you were thinking it. You looked at me, remember? That look, like, See?

So I looked *at you!* One time.

Lots of times. For lots of things.

You did the same to me! But so what, that's how we are. We know each other, we don't need to talk about it, we don't need to say all of the mean things in our heads. It's not constant. Once a week, twice a week . . . the rest of the time, everything is good. Was good. Before this.

Because a girl died, Amanda. She died. *This isn't a game anymore. We're not even the next time I forget to pick up a kid from the library.*

What good does it do? What good does it do? Nothing will bring her back to life; what good does it do to hate me?

It could have been Jenna. It was somebody else's Jenna.

I know. I know. Don't you think I know that? What do you think I'm thinking about at night, alone in the kitchen, with the goddam bottle of wine? But I can't change that. I can't change it. So if I'm going to change me, if I'm going to stop drinking, if we're going to make things better . . . then I just have to stop. I just have to stop thinking about that day. About the gas pedal and the car that came from out of nowhere. About how my shoe could have hit the brake. Should have hit the brake. How if only I had realized my mistake a second *sooner, just a second sooner.*

I can't stop thinking about it. Her parents can't stop thinking about that. Not ever. Why do we deserve to go back to our happy lives? When they can never get back to theirs?

She closes her eyes. She takes a deep breath and thinks again. This will not work. She cannot win this argument. Still standing at the doorway, she thinks again.

I'm sorry. I love you. I want this to work. Can you forgive me?

I'm sorry; I love you too. But I can't.

She closes her eyes again.

She thinks again.

Do you remember the time we took Matt and Jenna to SeaWorld? And we sat in the front row and we got completely drenched by the whales? The camera was ruined. The kids were shrieking and laughing and I was distraught because all of the pictures I had taken were probably destroyed, and you squeezed my hand and you pointed

—not at the whales, but at the kids—and you said, "Look honey, you're missing it." I miss that; I want that back.

That was an illusion.

I remember *it*.

I remember on the drive home, we ran out of gas—

I warned you that the gas gauge was off—

—and you didn't speak to me for three states.

If you had just listened to me in the first place . . .

Like I said, it was an illusion.

She lets her head rest on the doorframe, just for a moment. This will not work. This will not work. She has been over a thousand conversations in her head and she never wins.

In the back of her mind she hears Renata saying, *It can't possibly go as bad as you are imagining*, but Renata has never said that.

She cannot stand to let things just go on the way they have been, and she is powerless to fix things. It is all up to Sam. She does not like this feeling. Not being in charge, not being able to sweep up the mess, glue the robot's head back on, put the blocks back where they go.

She has to let go.

She thinks about how she can't let go; this is her family. She can't not fight for her family. That whole, "If you love something, set it free" thing is bull. What if it doesn't come back, what then?

But hasn't she already lost them? All that's left is getting them back.

She is still debating it when the door opens.

Sam jumps back in surprise.

He says nothing, just adjusts his glasses.

She licks her lips. They are standing in the narrow hallway, so close she can almost feel his breath on her face.

"Your phone was going off," she says, "this morning, the

alarm. You were in the shower already, and I went to shut it off. That woman, Susanna. You were texting her."

He says nothing. He looks down and shifts from foot to foot. His eyebrows arch as he notices her suitcase.

"Are you sleeping with her?" The easiest question first.

"No," he says quickly, looking up briefly to meet her eyes.

She lets out her breath.

"We haven't even kissed."

She feels her chest constrict.

"Are . . . are you in love with her?"

"I . . ." He looks to her side, past her, to the wall, as if fascinated by something. "I don't know." His mouth twitches. "I don't think so. I've just needed somebody. Someone to talk to."

At least he is talking. This is the most substantive thing he has said to her in weeks.

You could talk to me, she thinks.

No, he says in her mind. *I need someone to talk to about you.*

She swallows hard.

"Are you still in love with me?" she asks, looking away, past him to the aging history books on his shelves. Down to her feet. To his feet, his brown loafers, still shifting side to side but beginning to blur. She clenches her hands into fists and digs her fingernails into her palms.

He says nothing.

She thinks about the way they used to stay up into the night, talking about all they planned to do, how many kids they were going to have, the great jobs they would get, the great trips they would take. She thinks about the first night they brought Matt home, how exhausted they were, and how little they slept, because they kept getting up to feel through the darkness to his chest, to make sure it was still moving. She thinks about the grueling night they had after Jenna broke her leg going down a slide when she was three. How they lay with her between them, Jenna alternately whimpering and screaming no matter how much Tylenol they gave her. How they patted her back and caressed her face, and how, just as the room was beginning to brighten and the moon fading into the paling sky, she finally fell asleep. Then the alarm on Sam's watch beeped. They looked at each other and laughed. He met her eyes and whispered, "I love you."

She thinks about how you know you've reached the end when you can't look forward, only back.

She thinks about how they'll have to sit down with the kids tomorrow, or maybe the next day.

But not now. Now she would only cry. Sam can make up a story tonight.

She thinks about how she should say something.

But then, they were never any good at that.

Trembling, she lifts the suitcase.

"I'm sorry," he says, meeting her eyes.

"Me too," she whispers.

And then she turns and walks out the door.

4

PRECIOUS CASTAWAYS

At first, I avoid them. My father, who never thought I was as good as her. Sophie, his girlfriend, a.k.a. Chloe's mother, who just looks so goddamned sad at the funeral. I don't need that shit.

I mean, I'm not a bitch about it. No one could say, *Jade lived down to all the things they say about her*. I don't show up to the funeral drunk or stoned or skip it entirely. I come, I dress nicely. I even take out my piercings, that's how goddamn much I don't want to create a scene. I hug Sophie. I tell my dad I'm sorry for his loss. I charge a fruit basket to the "emergency" credit card my mom sometimes gives me when she's feeling guilty. Not just a "sorry for your loss" generic fruit basket. I put time into it; I find a website that will customize baskets, pick out their favorite fruits, avoiding kiwi fruit—even though it looks good and they both like it—because Chloe loved it, and I think it might bring up memories. I give them standard-issue fruits that won't spark memories and a few weird things that they won't associate with Chloe: strawberries, raspberries, mango, pineapple, watermelon, jujubes (yes, it turns out they are a fruit), lychee, and starfruit.

I skip blueberries because my dad is allergic to them,

apples because they don't look good, oranges because Sophie hates the white parts, and bananas because Chloe had eaten bananas on her oatmeal that morning.

After the funeral, though, I go home, back to my mom's. As if nothing ever happened.

I don't really know what to do with myself. I feel trapped in the middle of a shitstorm. I'd say this whole thing has divided our town, except it hasn't. No one thought much of Sophie and my dad before this, but now basically the whole town has lined up behind them, ready and eager to support them. On the other side of things, there is just the other driver, the drunk being charged with manslaughter . . . my aunt Amanda.

My mother told me this with pursed lips, late at night, the day of the accident. "We stick by family," she added, even though Amanda is only related by marriage. This was after she "casually" mentioned that she would be picking up all of my aunt's legal fees.

"Which family?" I asked her.

She stared at me blankly. "Oh, c'mon, Jade," she said. "Your father never gave a damn about you. They're not even married, you hardly ever go over there; you didn't even like Chloe."

I was silently astonished that she knew I didn't like Chloe. She must have listened to me ranting at one point. Maybe it seeped in by osmosis.

"I spend a lot of time there," I said, finding the one thing I could take issue with. "Where do you think I sleep when you kick me out?"

"Oh, honestly, Jade, it's not like I change the locks," she said, half-rolling her eyes to stare up at the ceiling. She ran a hand through her perfect brown bob. She looks nothing like me; I'm adopted, a mail-order Chinese baby whose original parents decided she had come out wrong, missing the all-important Y chromosome. "It's not like they have a bedroom for you," she added. "And I know you spend at least half those nights at Sam and Amanda's. They, at least, have the courtesy to call and tell me you're not lying dead on the streets."

Sam and Amanda are my aunt and uncle.

I couldn't argue much of that, so I said, "I'm sorry, am I misinterpreting, *Get the hell out of my house! I don't want to see you around here until you shape the hell up!?*"

"Clearly," she said, with a shake of her head, her arms pushing at the air as if to cast me out. "Seeing as you never do shape the hell up."

If things were different with us, I probably would have laughed. But she didn't give me a chance, getting up and stalking out of the room.

After Chloe dies, there are two things I do that I am not proud of. The first is that I hide out at my mother's house, even when she pisses me off. I don't even visit Sophie and Dad.

When the guidance counselor, who is "talking to all of those who may have been affected by the tragedy" asks me how my dad and Sophie are doing, I lie and say, "You know, hanging on," like I actually know how they are doing.

The second thing that I do that I am not proud of is that, to avoid the other side as well, I stop eating lunch with my cousin Matt, Aunt Amanda's son.

"What's up with lunch?" he asks me the first day, cornering me by my locker.

I just shrug. "Changing things up. Got bored of the lame conversation, you know."

He narrows his eyes. I never noticed before how much they look like his dad's. Like my mom's. "Seriously, Jade, I thought you were better than this. How the hell would you like it if people judged you based on what your mom did?"

"It's not that," I promise him. I pull on my lower lip with my fingernail, right in the spot that I might like to pierce it one day. "David was sitting all alone . . ." I shrug.

Matt's eyes stop narrowing, and he no longer looks so much like my mother. "Were they close?" he asks.

David is—was—Chloe's half-brother. Same dad, different moms. Never lived together or anything. But still . . .

I want to say no, because they kind of hated each other, but it feels like a betrayal. "I don't know," I say. "I was with him, when it happened. When he saw her being loaded into the ambulance or whatever. He needs me around to like, distract him and stuff."

"I need you around to distract me." Matt can be whiny when he wants to be. A side effect of having parents who actually notice when you're unhappy and try to fix things. He walks though life expecting people to be nice and help him out and whatnot.

"You still have Cam and all of the photography geeks and probably Cassie," I tell him, throwing my head back and letting out a purposely loud sigh. "David was sitting all alone."

"OK," he says, shifting his weight from one foot to another. "You're off the hook for lunch. But I still expect to hang with you, like before."

"Sure," I say.

It is all a lie. Or mostly a lie. Yes, I felt bad for David. But also, I didn't want to sit with Matt. I didn't want to pretend that every time I saw him, I didn't think about how his mom, my semi-beloved aunt Amanda, killed Chloe. I make a million mistakes, but even I know you call for a goddamn ride.

I may not have liked Chloe, but she would still be alive if my aunt hadn't been so colossally self-centered.

It won't be like before. I won't go over to his basement to hang, or to crash when my mom kicks me out, or to practice for the punk band we sort of have with Cam, one of Matt's friends. We never performed for anyone except my cousin

Jenna, and we were never any good, so it shouldn't be much of a loss.

But it is.

A few weeks after Chloe dies, my mom comes home while Vince, this guy I'm kind of seeing, and I are upstairs in my room, you know, hanging out and . . . stuff, and kicks us both out.

"What if Nina had walked in on you?!" she screams. Nina is my seven-year-old sister. "I don't ever want to see her doing this kind of thing! Both of you, out, now! Jade, goddamn it, get dressed first!"

Normally this is where I would go to Matt's house. His bedroom is in the basement, and in the main part of the basement, there is a couch. My couch, my home away from home. My aunt once offered to get a bed for me, to make one of their tiny offices into a bedroom of sorts. I declined. I like my couch. I especially like the fact that there is a second set of stairs leading to a storm shelter door. An escape, if I ever needed one. I like knowing I am free.

And I like Matt waking me up by kicking at the base of the couch. "Get your ass up; we've got school."

"I'll meet you there," I would tell him, pulling a pillow over my face.

"No," he'd say. "You are too smart to flunk out just because you couldn't be bothered to show up. You can sleep once you're there."

I would mutter something under my breath and get up and shower. Eat some of the waffles or pancakes or whatever it was my uncle made for breakfast (he was very into break-fast). Ride shotgun with Matt, forcing my cousin Jenna into the back seat. Stumble into class.

Now I don't know what to do. I don't want to go to my dad's.

After much deliberation, I decide to embrace being homeless and move into the park downtown.

In actuality, I just hang out at the dinky two-screen movie theater until the final picture finishes unspooling at one in the morning, dozing through multiple airings of the same stupid romantic comedy. Then I go to the park. The park isn't bad, it's just that it gets cold at night, this being late September and all, and I don't have space in my backpack for anything warmer than a sweatshirt. I curl up in one of the pipes they have set up as a tunnel on the playground and shiver. I tell myself it's like all of those camping trips my mother never took me on as a child. I tell myself that it will be a good story one day. I tell myself that I don't need anyone.

I sleep good, knowing that.

I keep eating lunch with David, plus Lacey, the new girl, who I dragged over to our table as well. Partially because David is depressing, and partially because she looks like she needs me and my awesome wisdom. And, you know, like they say, the more the merrier.

"Wow," Lacey says when she hears I am sleeping at the park. Her eyes go wide like she has never heard of anyone our age being homeless.

"It's no big deal," I tell her with a shrug.

Actually, it's pretty awesome, at least in that moment, because I don't need anyone.

Some afternoons we go over to David's and hang out. His house offers heat, cable TV, and a relaxed attitude toward marijuana. On the downside, the place is a mess, with cobwebs forming under the TV, pizza boxes covering the kitchen table, and spent cigarette butts cluttering the end table. His mother sometimes wanders around, as if in a daze. If you try to use the microwave while the washing machine is running, it blows a fuse.

"You can always crash here," he offers. "I mean, it's kind

of a mess, but . . ."

"Your house is awesome," I tell him. "I just, you know, I like sleeping at the park. All that fresh air. Nature and stuff. And it's great preparation for when I move to the city and become a street performer."

"Something could happen out there," he mutters. I don't know if he means the park or the city. He is moving a joint in-between his fingers, not taking a hit, just staring at it.

I reach over and wrest it away from him. "I'll be fine," I tell him when he looks up at me. "I can take care of myself."

Still, in mid-October, when I decide that I have proven that I don't need any favors or a place to sleep, David's is the first place I go in my quest for warmer accommodations.

No one minds if I crash, which is nice, and there is, surprisingly, usually something edible in the fridge.

I sleep on the couch, but I wake up at two in the morning to find him curled in the Lay-Z-Boy, watching the news, of all things.

"Sorry," he says. "I tried to keep the volume down."

The first rule about couch surfing is you respect the natives. "It's cool," I tell him, lighting a cigarette.

"We can change it to something else if you want."

"Oh, no," I say, inhaling deeply. "I've always wondered what bacteria could be lurking in public bathrooms. Why watch a horror flick when there's CNN?"

He doesn't crack a smile, just stares at the TV, eyes wide, jaw clenched.

"This sort of stuff will really keep you up all night," I say, after the segment ends.

"Yeah," he says. "Sorry."

"It's fascinating," I tell him. "I wonder if they'll do an exposé on those restaurant mints after the break."

"Already done," he says, eyes never leaving the TV. "They sent them to a lab or something. Really gross. They got footage of people leaving the bathroom without washing their hands, then sticking them in the bowl of mints."

"Gross," I echo, even though I already know this story.

He shrugs. "I don't really care about that stuff. They're supposed to get to international stuff soon."

"War, disease, terrorism?"

"Pretty much."

"Thrilling."

He changes over to Comedy Central. "It's fine," I tell him, stubbing out my cigarette. "We can watch the news."

"No one likes the news," he says, eyes never breaking from the TV.

After a week of that, I move around. Don't want to wear out my welcome and all. First I try crashing at Vince's, which is nice and warm and cozy, but then his stepmom catches us and says it's not appropriate. I don't want to get into things, so I don't mention being sort of homeless. She's the type who would try to do something about it, and I don't need that. My shrink from two years ago called Social Services on us, and my mom freaked out and told her, "She is always welcome at home. She just doesn't come home some nights. Yes, maybe you could recommend a good program. Outward Bound, perhaps."

Then I try Cam's, but Matt finds out about it and gives me the saddest look.

"You know we have a couch with your name on it," he says to me, stopping me at the salad bar in the cafeteria. "Like, literally."

I once carved my name on the underside of the bottom slat of the couch with a steak knife. I can't remember why I did it; I think sometimes I just do things. *Poor impulse control*, my former shrink would say.

"Sorry," I mutter. I look away from him. Study the orange

and black crepe paper someone has mounted to the bottom of the cafeteria counters in honor of the upcoming holiday.

"It's not my fault," he says.

"I know . . ." I try to reach my arm out, to touch his shoulder or something like they would do on TV, but he walks away.

And still I can't bring myself to go back there.

As it happens, the new guidance counselor pulls me into her office again that afternoon.

"Just checking in," she says. "Your attendance has been better."

I don't tell her that school is warm and has hot meals and I am homeless, so I sort of need these things. I just nod.

She drops her voice and looks deep into my eyes. "How are your father and Sophie?" she asks.

My stomach twists.

"You know, holding together," I say, like I actually know how they are doing. I feel like a piece of shit.

And I feel like a piece of shit about so many things, I just can't take any more. So I go over there, after school. Just kind of casually open the door to the apartment, plunk down my backpack, and take off my sweatshirt.

Sophie is on the couch, under a crocheted afghan that her grandmother or somebody made—the kind of thing that looks godawful with orange and green and brown done up in squares, but which was clearly made *with love*. There is no box of tissues next to her and no trashcan to hold them, which is a good sign.

The TV is off, though.

She looks up at me and tries what I think is a smile. There is a twitch in the corner of her mouth, anyway.

Her face is not streaked with tears or mascara, but then again, she is not wearing makeup. She looks older without it. Her skin is blotchy; there are dark circles beneath her eyes, and wrinkles on her forehead and at the corners of her mouth and eyes. She is only thirty-five, ten years younger than my mother, but she looks older right now. Her dark curly hair is unwashed, greasy, tangled.

But there is no backing out the door now. I'm not that big of a bitch.

"Hi," I say. I don't know what to do with my mouth. Or feet. Or hands. I twitch into a half-smile, rock from one foot to the other, scratch at my left hand with my right.

"Are you staying?" she asks.

I can't tell if she wants me to or not. I suddenly realize that I might remind them of Chloe—being a sixteen-year-old girl and all—but then I figure everything reminds them of Chloe. Why not pile it on?

I shrug.

"Did you have a fight with your mother?" she asks.

"Nothing new," I say.

She shakes her head back and forth, as if to clear it. "How are you?" she asks.

"Goo—" I start to say, then realize how incredibly insulting it is to be doing well when they are utterly devastated. Or *she* is utterly devastated. I can never tell with my father.

"You know," I say. I shrug again. How can I say I am doing fine? That it hasn't even touched me? That I am a cold, soulless person, that I hated her daughter, that the death that has devastated her has not wrenched my heart in two?

She nods.

"Do you want some tea?" I ask. She looks like she could use tea. A cold front has come through; the light outside the single window in the living room is gray; the 45-degree chill is settling into the apartment. My father, the cheap bastard, is probably insisting they don't turn on the heat.

She nods. "Yes," she says.

I go into the kitchen. I breathe in and out a few times.

Sophie is the type of person who owns a teapot, so I fill it with water and set it on the stove. Of course, for all I know, my mother owns a teapot, but has written it off as "inefficient," compared with nuking water, and stashed it somewhere in the attic.

I set up two cups and rummage through the pantry. Everything is just where it was before.

I pick out Earl Gray, caffeinated. Maybe with some caffeine she will sit up.

I get the mugs ready—basic white ones, not the rose-colored ones that Chloe always liked.

The pot whistles sooner than I'd like, and I pour the steaming water into the mugs. Breathe it in.

Spoon in some sugar—we both like sugar—and carry them out into the living room, doing my best impression of a waitress who can balance more than one cup while walking.

I set a mug in front of her on the coffee table, then curl into the rocking chair.

She sits up, keeping the afghan wrapped around her.

She wraps her fingers around the mug. Steam wafts off of it.

"That is nice," she says.

I nod.

"What is new with you?" she asks.

I shrug.

"I have not been back to work," she says, a bit of her old-world accent coming through. Her family moved here from one of those little tiny countries that keep changing their name when she was in high school. "I think I will lose my job. Or maybe I have already lost it. I do not know. They said they would hold it, but . . . I don't think they meant forever."

"That sucks," I say.

Sophie works technical support for the cable company. All those commercials where they try to reassure you that their tech support lives next door and not in India—that's her.

Except that the actors they hired to portray her don't live anywhere around here.

Sophie shrugs. "Your father is paying for everything now. And they keep cutting his hours. I don't know . . ."

"There should be something for that," I say. "Like, disability or whatever. I mean, what do they expect you to do?"

"Be strong," she says. She swallows hard, then takes a sip of tea. "It is probably what I should do. I am just lazy now. When I was a girl, there was no space for laziness. No space to sit and think about everything. Now, though, I am soft."

"You deserve a break," I say. "You need some space."

"No," she says. "I need to be busy. But I cannot manage it. I think, *Today I will get up. Today I will go out. Today I will call Kelly and see if they still have a place for me. Today I will buy groceries.*" She shrugs her shoulders together. "Then I do not. And then the next day it is just a little bit harder."

I have no good advice. I am a sixteen-year-old deadbeat.

"I've heard that, like, wallowing is supposed to be good. Psychologically and such," I offer.

"No," she says. "Wallowing is lying in the muck. The earth sucking you down. You need to get up on dry land, put one foot in front of the other until you get back into some place you recognize."

I nod. Sip my tea.

"Ha," she snorts. "I have all of the wisdom and it means nothing; I know I need to get up, and yet . . ." She waves her arm across the room, palm up.

Adults, outside of my parents, like to talk to me like this. Like I am a person. Matt says it's something about my aura. They figure they don't have to watch their language around me; they figure they can actually tell me whatever is in their heads. Because I've seen it all, clearly.

"Enough about me," she says with a sigh. "You and your mother are fighting again?"

"We never stop." I shrug. "I had a guy over. That's her reasoning, anyway . . . things were getting tense already. It was only a matter of time before something blew up."

"Do you like this boy?" she asks. "What is his name?"

"I guess," I say. "Yeah. Vince."

"How long have you been seeing him?" she asks.

"A couple of months," I say. We hooked up at the beginning of summer.

"You are being safe?" she says.

"Yeah, we know all that."

"And with your heart?"

"No one can touch me," I say, cocking my head slightly. "I'm always safe."

"Maybe you need to be less safe then," she says.

I laugh, then try quickly to wipe away the smile.

Her lips have relaxed, though, and there is almost a smile there.

"Are you two serious?" she asks.

I shrug. All I do is shrug.

"You like a boy, you should be exclusive," she says. "I know, I know, you know better than me, all you young people. But you know I say this from experience."

"I know," I say. That's the reason Chloe and David are —*were*—half-siblings. Their dad wasn't exactly committed.

The problem is, being exclusive involves a conversation. *Do you want to be exclusive?* Note that there is only one right answer. *Have you been exclusive up until now?* Still, only one right answer. *What does being exclusive mean?* Well, it means we have to care about each other. It means I have to listen, or do a better job of pretending, when you talk about whatever it is that you're into. It means I'm supposed to see you, like, every friggin' day.

Then, later, we have to have the other conversation. *It's not you, it's me.* Which means we can't go back to just hanging out, and we can't go back to me sleeping over without even putting out, and we can't go back to anything, really.

"Ah, you will do whatever you want," she says, but not all passive-aggressive like my father. More like she's winking at me.

We spend the afternoon watching trashy TV and occasionally commenting on how ridiculous it all is. Things are pleasant.

Then my father gets home.

"Haven't seen you in a while." That is the first thing he says. He is short and stocky and starting to go bald. I don't know what Sophie sees in him. She is one of the nicest people I know, and he is just an ass.

"Been busy," I mutter.

"Jade and I have had a very nice afternoon visiting," Sophie says, an edge to her voice.

My father sighs and runs a hand through his thinning hair. "It's nice to see you," he says, not meaning it. "You had a fight with your mother."

"She wanted to see us," Sophie lies for me.

I think I hear my father snort, but we all pretend he doesn't.

"You being safe?" he asks me. I don't know if that means he knows why my mother and I were fighting, which would be creepy, or if he just means in general, what with the homelessness and all.

"Always," I say.

He turns to Sophie. "Does this mean you're giving up the couch and coming to bed?" His eyebrows rise.

"Yes," she says simply. Then, "Jade, you should sleep in the bedroom, though." She waves her hand in the direction of the hallway. "No need to hurt your back on the couch. It is really getting too old. I think the springs may be going."

She means *her* bedroom. *Chloe's* bedroom.

"No," I say quickly. "I like the couch. It's near the TV."

The couch is twenty years old, give or take. It's brown and tan in some sort of pattern that is supposed to disguise stains. One of the springs always pokes into my thigh. It will be a thousand times more comfortable than Chloe's silver-canopy-topped Sealy Posturepedic.

Dinner is weird, quiet. Chloe is not bubbling along, yammering on about some friend or some guy, or some after-school activity. My father stabs at microwaved beans in silence. Sophie pushes her food around the plate like an anorexic, barely eating anything at all.

I, on the other hand, eat it all. My mother does not cook, doesn't even microwave, and when I'm without a home base, I subsist off of Doritos and chocolate milk, so while this isn't up to Sophie's usual standard, it's the best food I've had in ages.

"How's school?" my father asks. I notice that he's lost weight, probably due to the lack of Sophie's cooking. He was never fat, just plump, but now he's looking almost normal, maybe five or ten pounds overweight, which itself is normal at his age.

"Fine."

"You going?" His face looks red. It always looks red. What's left of his hair sticks out as being paler than the rest of him.

"Bob," Sophie starts.

"No, I've decided to drop out and try my fortune as a street performer," I say. "So far I can only juggle one knife at a time, and it has to be a plastic one. Do you think that will take away from my tips?"

My father snorts, and not a nice kind of snort.

"She is going," Sophie says. "Lay off of her."

"Yes," I echo. "School provides me with shelter and food. I'd live there if they let me."

"What the hell?" he says. He points a chubby index finger

at my plate. "Food." He raises his palm toward the ceiling. "Shelter."

"That's kind of why I'm here."

"You maybe want to ask us how we're doing?"

"Bob—"

"Sure, Dad, how are you doing? Crappy? I'm shocked. Terribly sorry to hear that. So glad I asked."

My father rises, face redder than usual. "You cannot even begin to imagine what we are going through," he says. "You live in your little bubble. . . . Sophie can barely eat or sleep. . . . But no, your little teenage drama . . . "

"Bob," Sophie says.

He shakes his head, rises, and carries his glass to the sink. I watch his back move as he angrily washes the glass and places it in the dish rack. He leaves the room without a backward glance.

"Don't mind him," Sophie says. She rises too, and clears his plate.

"You shouldn't have to do that," I say.

She shrugs. "He is having a hard time. And he does not get the luxury of, what was the word, *wallowing*."

"Right," I say, wondering what, exactly, his excuse was before.

After Sophie is finished pushing her food around her plate, we sit on the couch and watch sitcoms.

"Everything on the TV is so easy," she says.

"No," I say. "You just have to spring for a better package. AMC, HBO. Their lives are all completely screwed."

"Yes," she says. "Depressingly real television. That is exactly what I need."

I laugh, just for a second.

She smiles, I think.

Later on, she takes a deep breath, says good night, and pads off to the bedroom, afghan clutched around her shoulders.

I think that she and my dad probably have not had sex since Chloe died.

I hope that they do tonight, although I *so* don't want to hear it. Of course, Sophie's hair is unkempt and her skin is sagging, so I think that they will probably just lie with their backs to each other, offering more cold than warmth, and wander along in their own thoughts until one or the other of them starts to snore.

Me, I sleep well. It's warm and I have blankets from the hall closet. The green, gender-neutral guest ones, not the pink and purple ones Chloe always liked.

I wonder, if I slept in Chloe's room, if Sophie would awake at night to use the bathroom, and catch a glimpse of the lump, and forget, just for a moment.

I wake up early. To be nice, I leave a note. *Hitting the bakery before school.*

They will either be offended that I just slipped out or shocked that I am actually getting up on my own in the morning. And by "they" I really just mean my father.

After hitting the bakery with the emergency credit card, I set up camp in front of Matt's locker.

He shows up five minutes before the first bell. "You suck," he says.

"I got up early for you, Matty."

"Will miracles never cease." He reaches past me to turn the knob on his combination lock.

"It's not you, Matt. You know it's not you."

He waits, hand suspended on the lock.

"Sorry," I mutter, kicking at the tiled floor with my boot.

When he ignores me, I take a deep breath and try again, looking at him this time. "I'm really fucking sorry."

His hands shake slightly in the cold. "Why can't everything just go back to the way it was?" He looks like he is about to cry. Normally I would tell him to man up, but I feel bad, and he is still slightly pissed at me, so I give him a hug.

"We should hang out more," I say. "I want to hang out with you. You're family. It's just . . . not at your house. The park, maybe?"

"I guess," he mutters. "She hardly ever comes downstairs, you know. You could sneak in and avoid her."

I shrug.

"You could just man up and deal with her," he says, eyebrow raised.

I smile and stick my tongue out at him.

The bell rings, and Matt is a creature of habit. I hand him his breakfast and he shuffles off to class with the rest of the sheep.

I go back to Sophie's after school. I don't want her to feel like I abandoned her. And also because I genuinely like spending time with Sophie, at least until my dad gets home and I start to feel like maybe I'm causing more issues than I'm fixing.

My father and I were never close. He met my mom in high school, which is always a surefire way to have an unhappy marriage. He followed her around like a puppy, changing cities and jobs as she worked her way through undergrad, med school, and a residency near their hometown. They adopted me when she was doing her residency, because, sure, a time when you have to work thirty-six hours straight is the perfect time to add a nine-month-old to the picture.

And this is where things fell apart. Because my dad was suddenly supposed to be the woman in the relationship: take care of the baby, do the dishes, make life easier on my mom. His twice-minimum-wage job at the Home Depot was mean- ingless, unnecessary stacked up against my mother's future earnings potential. He was supposed to quit and devote himself to providing a nice, clean environment and a nice, clean kid for her to come home to.

He lasted six months.

My mom replaced him with a cleaning service, plus my aunt Amanda, who was taking a hiatus from real estate to raise Matt. As far as I can tell, Aunt Amanda was a definite upgrade from my dad. She read to us and fed us organic purees and had us make little art projects out of construction paper and cotton balls.

I was better off, even if she did eventually, you know, kill someone.

I stay at Sophie's for a week, to be polite. Then I suck it up and go back home. My sister Nina, at least, is happy to see me.

"Why do you and mom fight all the time?" she asks one night while Mom is working late.

"I was never meant to live with her," I say after a moment.

"I'm adopted, too. We get along."

I want to tell her that when I was her age, I got along with Mom, too.

"You're a different personality," I tell her. "You're the kind of personality she would have gotten if she could get pregnant. Me, I'm different."

She stares at me some more.

"It's OK," I tell her. "Mom and I will get along really well once I move out. We're just not supposed to, like, share a space."

"I don't want you to move out."

"I can't move out yet," I tell her. "And when I do, you can come hang out at my place."

"Can I stay over if Mom works late?"

"Of course," I lie. Mom will probably never let her set foot in my apartment, let alone spend the night. But Nina doesn't need to worry about that now.

. . .

Matt starts coming over after school on the days I don't hang out with David and Lacey. Mostly to complain about his life, which gets tiring.

"My parents don't even fight," he says, pacing back and forth across the rec room. "They just don't say a goddamn word. It's strangling me."

"Then do something about it," I tell him. I am sitting cross-legged on the couch, a Zen Buddha. Now that he has forgiven me, my patience has quickly waned.

He stares at me. "I know you don't want to, but you should come over. You're good at just telling people what's what. Maybe you can—"

I stop him, my hand up, palm out. My black sparkle nails shimmer at me.

"Matt," I tell him, massaging my temples, "I'm not going over there. I'm not fixing it. I'm sorry. I love you and I love your family and all, but . . . I can't forgive her. I can't fix her life and make things better for her. I can't even look at her." I can't look at him.

He stops pacing and stares at me. I finally look back, deep into his brown eyes. "You wouldn't be doing it for her."

"Matt," I say, rising out of my seat, "It's time you grew a pair and stopped whining and went in there yourself. Tell them to deal with it, or see a shrink—I'm sure my mother would be happy to pay for one and remind them of it every year at Christmas—or, you know, whatever. Or, if you don't have the balls to go talk to them, then go out and do something crazy, like get a tattoo over your eye or one grab of those high school dropout forms and leave it laying around the kitchen or something so maybe they figure all of their crap is affecting you and decide to do something. But, like, whining about it is just not going to do anything."

He is quiet for a long time. "Fine," he says, sinking into the sofa in defeat. "But you whine a lot too."

"I am as God made me," I say with a shrug.

And, because he is not my mother, he smiles.

For the next few weeks, I go over on Mondays and Thursdays to see Sophie. I make her tea and offer to do her nails or cut her hair. She says OK, and I start to make her look like a person again.

I usually leave before my dad gets home, unless I'm really hungry. Sophie makes a crock-pot stew one day—frozen veggies and potatoes, but real meat that I help her pick out at the store—so I stay for that.

Ten days before Thanksgiving, I help Nina put green streaks in her hair.

"Is Mom going to be mad?" she asks.

"I don't see why," I tell her. "You look awesome. It really stands out against black hair."

Of course, that gets me kicked out again.

It's too cold to go back to the park, so I settle into a routine. I go to Sophie's after school, have a snack, and then I go out with my lunch friends until Lacey has to go home and David starts to look too sad.

If he's in an OK headspace, I sometimes crash at David's. Otherwise, I wander around town for a bit, maybe see a movie, maybe sip coffee at the café, anything to kill the time until I'm pretty sure my father is in bed. Then I go back to Sophie's.

If I guess wrong, my father glares at me and says something like, "I'm sorry, did I miss the sign that says this hotel has a twenty-four hour check-in policy?"

I say, "If it was a hotel, there would be room service."

"You need to watch your mouth," he says, because he can't think of anything better to say. "And your waistline."

There are a number of things I could say here. *Pot calling the kettle,* but that's too clever. *Fuck you,* but that demands a dramatic exit, back into the cold. *You wish I were dead instead of her,* but that kind of insightful, cloying sadness is just for people on TV.

So I just say, "Sure, Dad, if you let me use your bathroom, I'll go vomit up dinner."

And because Sophie is glaring at him, he shuts up and says he is really sorry and he was out of line with as much genuine emotion as is possible for him.

I don't know what to do about Thanksgiving. My mother always has my cousins over. Aunt Amanda usually cooks, but Nina tells me Mom is having a pre-made meal delivered this year, as Aunt Amanda doesn't seem up to cooking.

I can't go there.

I also can't go to my father's, because that would be, what? A slap in the face? A giant middle finger? I would gladly give that to my mother, but I still weirdly like my screw-up aunt more than her, and that just seems like adding insult to injury. Plus, there is Matt, all sensitive to that kind of stuff.

Besides, I don't want to have to talk to my dad.

I catch Lacey at her locker the day before Thanksgiving.

"Hey, Lace," I ask, "can you invite me over for dinner tomorrow?"

She stares at me blankly. She's the quiet type, but easy to get along with. Plus, I figure her mom knows how to cook.

"For Thanksgiving?" I say. "I don't exactly want to be around my dad, but I don't want to be rude to Sophie. And I definitely don't want to be at my mom's. So if my friend invited me over for dinner . . ."

"It's not going to be any fun," she says. Her mouth twists around in this funny way. I'm sure I've made her uncomfortable, which is fine. I often make people uncomfortable.

"It won't involve your mom telling me I'm fat, lazy, and pathetic, right?"

Her eyebrows scrunch together. "Probably not . . ." I want to hug her.

I grin at her instead. "So am I invited?"

"I guess . . ." I am sure she is going to have fun explaining this one to her mother.

"Thanks! You're the best!" I give her a quick hug and then race down the hall before she can reconsider.

My mom sends me about a hundred texts about Thanksgiving and my selfish, childish nature. Sophie sends me a *Happy Thanksgiving! Do you have somewhere to eat?* text, because she's nice like that. More guilt, because I should be eating with her. Lacey's quiet at dinner, so I have to talk a lot. Her mom seems interested in that way that people get when they're driving past a freeway accident.

My life exists to be gawked at.

On the plus side, I have warmth and food.

Two weeks later, my aunt moves out of her home. Which means we just had our last Thanksgiving. And I missed it.

"It's messed up," Matt tells me through ragged breath while we sit on park bench still damp from the snow we'd hastily brushed off. "My dad tells us that she's going to a retreat or something for a few days. I figure it's a cover for rehab or something—she'd started drinking a lot. Then she comes home the next day—they clearly didn't coordinate at all—and tells us she's sorry, but she's moving out. Better for everyone.

"What she means is, better for her," he continues. "Two weeks before Christmas. Two weeks. They couldn't even hold it together that long."

"I'm sorry," I tell him. There is nothing else to say. *I should have been there. I should have fixed it for you.* I suck.

Now I really don't want to go there for Christmas, and I feel like a piece of crap. And I don't want to go to my dad's and be told how much I suck. Lacey can't exactly invite me over for

Christmas. I am trying to figure out what to do when I come home to Sophie's one Friday after school, just a week before Christmas—snow stuck between the grooves in my combat boots and pounded into ice—and find the rocking chair and TV gone. I find Sophie in the kitchen, scrubbing.

"What happened?" I ask.

"He is gone," she says. "I kicked him out."

"Oh," I say.

"You help me in here; then we do her room," she says. "Then you have a proper bed to sleep in."

"No," I say.

"Yes," she says. "I cannot look at it anymore. I cannot see that closed door one more goddamn day. I cannot live with a ghost anymore."

"I don't want to stay there," I say. "You don't have to worry about me."

"We tackle the kitchen, I have a glass of wine, then we do her room," she says. It is not a question.

"OK," I say.

I throw out old food, boxes of cake with worms, stuff in the fridge that has turned to brown sludge. She comes behind me with a scrubbing sponge and wipes up all of the sludge that has oozed everywhere.

We are quiet. We don't quite coordinate, but it all gets done.

The kitchen is old and falling apart, and some of the tiles don't match, but now it is clean.

At Chloe's door, I take a deep breath.

Sophie crosses herself, which is funny because she isn't Catholic, and twists the knob and plunges in.

It smells like springtime.

It looks just like it always did. Purple walls, faux-oak dresser, silver canopy bed with pink trim.

Pictures, pictures, everywhere. Her and her hundreds of friends, smiling and looking all-American. Her and her dad or her and her half-brothers in bathing suits, squinting on a beach. Her and Sophie, looking so very much alike, Sophie's eyes older, her smile more weary; Chloe, young and innocent and full of life.

She had just had sex with her football player boyfriend before she died, or so David said. She had been upset about something, asking their older brother for advice. It had seemed like juicy gossip at the time. I'm not sure it matters now. She will always be young and innocent and virginal. A perfect smiling face on the wall.

I throw the perfume into a trash bag. The pictures go into a shoebox.

I open the drawers while Sophie strips the bed.

"The clothes we can donate," she says.

"Do you want to keep anything?" I ask.

"So I can curl in a ball and breathe in her scent and cry myself to sleep?" she says. "No, no, I keep the pictures, but that is enough. I can cry the rest of my life on memories, on what I see when I close my eyes. I do not need those pictures even. But, then I cannot let them go, so those I will keep. Everything else, everything else goes."

There are trophies for cheerleading and such. I think about the first time our parents introduced us. We were twelve.

"Oh yeah, I've seen you around school," she said. "Didn't we have third grade together?"

"I've suppressed all memories of third grade," I told her. "It was a very traumatic year."

She stared at me, an eyebrow cocked. "Do you want to see my room?"

"Sure," I said, trying to make sure my lack of enthusiasm came through. "That will be thrilling."

"Our middle school cheer squad won last year," she said, showing me the trophy.

"Won for what? Screaming the loudest?"

"There's actually a lot of acrobatics," she said, voice still way too bright.

"And what better way to use those talents than to cheer on the boys," I said.

She stared at me, not getting it.

"What do you want to do with them?" I ask Sophie, holding up one of the trophies. It's painted gold and features a girl, presumably airborne, arms and legs spread into Vs.

"Toss them," Sophie says.

I delicately place each castaway statue into the white drawstring trash bag.

Her lipstick goes into the trash.

Her nail polish. Pinks and purples and greens. And a red that she probably hadn't used since the day in ninth grade when I told her, "You look like a hooker."

"You would know," she said, not missing a beat. If nothing else, exposure to me had made her much quicker on the draw. "I hear you gave a guy a blow job for a cigarette."

It wasn't true. I was still a virgin at that point. But that certainly wasn't something I wanted her to know.

"A carton," I said. "I never settle for anything less than a carton."

The plastic horses she kept from her childhood go in the donation box. So does her jewelry, the faux silver stuff her dad and boyfriends would buy for her.

The books, mostly romance and teen vampire trash, get donated. In the closet there are boxes of letters; from friends, from boys, from her dad.

"I don't know," Sophie says. "Toss them. They will just make it harder."

I think about all the things on them. Gossip, devotions of love, mean words, apologies. Things people wanted her to know. Responses to things she'd said.

Things that meant enough for her to keep.

When Sophie is not looking, I put them in my backpack. I don't know why; if I am some sick voyeur pawing through a dead girl's things, or if I will just keep them, unread, just so that this little part of her doesn't disappear. Or maybe it is just my *poor impulse control* shining through.

"It will get better," I tell Sophie, without the faintest bit of experience.

"No," she says. "I should be an adult and lie to you, but I am too tired. I will get used to it; that is all. I will wait and I will wait and eventually I will learn to get used to it. You can learn to get used to anything."

Her eyes look tired, sunken, hollow. Her jaw is slack, her limbs dangle. She reaches back into the closet for another box.

This, I think. This is why I can't even look at my aunt Amanda. The woman who was more of a mother to me than my own mother. Not because of what she did to Chloe, but because of what she did to Sophie. If there were sides to pick, then I picked mine.

"That's pretty dark," I tell Sophie.

"What?" she says. "You think only young people are full of darkness?" She arches her eyebrows at me.

"No," I say. What else is there to say? No one I ever knew has died, except for a great-grandmother I met once and Chloe, who I never liked.

"We are all damaged," she says. But she is broken and in traction, and all I have is a paper cut.

I wait for her to say something about survival or hope, even. Or just moving on. About being happy again, some day.

But we're living in the world of pay cable, not network TV, and so she does not lie to me.

I think about one time when my dad was yelling at me and he looked over at Chloe and he said, "Now why can't you be more like Chloe? She's nice and pleasant, she gets good grades, and she keeps her legs closed."

"And when I jump off a cliff, you should totally jump off a cliff too," Chloe said, in full command of that bright, bubbly cheerleader voice.

My father stared at her, mouth agape. Then he shut it.

Chloe winked at me.

And all I did was glare. And give her the finger behind her back. Fuck her; I didn't need her help. I didn't need anyone.

And now she is gone.

And I never did like her. Not even once.

I wish she was here in this room; I wish she was here to hug Sophie and tell her everything will be OK. I wish she was here to make it all OK.

Instead, there is just me.

"We need a break," I tell Sophie. I reach over and squeeze her hand. I feel something start to stir behind my face, like it might just crack open. "I'll make us some tea."

Sophie looks deep into my eyes and runs a hand over my cheek. It is cool and warm all at once, and my mouth involuntarily cracks into something hideous looking. Sophie nods. She exhales and sinks down onto the floor while I turn, wipe at my face, and go to heat up water.

5

HOT AND COLD

Matt found it in January. Barely a month after his mom had moved out.

He and his sister were eating breakfast at the counter. She was leaned over, reading some sort of graphic novel. He listened to the *crunch, crunch, crunch* of her chewing her toast and wished he could say something.

He could think of nothing to say.

It was like that, these days. Long periods of silence, punctuated by inane chatter whenever he could think of a good subject.

Today, he was having trouble coming up with anything. So they crunched their breakfast in silence, his sister pawing through a comic book.

His father had gone down the hall to his office to grab something, or change a paragraph he'd just thought to change, or something. Matt hadn't been paying attention.

His father had left his phone lying on the lower side of the counter. It made a chirping sound.

Then another.

He couldn't say why he reached down and picked it up. He was sick of the silence; he was looking for something to do. He was hoping it was his mother, hoping to find out more than the little his parents had told them. Was she going to jail? Were they getting a divorce? Or was this just some rough patch, something that would get smoothed over in their collective memories with the passage of time?

He looked at the screen.

Had a great time last night
We should do that again

It was from a name he didn't recognize: Susanna.

He dropped the phone back down with a clatter.

"What was it?" his sister asked. She was wearing an over-sized black hoodie (no doubt borrowed from him) with the hood pulled forward around her red curls.

"Nothing," he said quickly. "Something about work. Picking up another section, I don't know."

Jenna shrugged and turned back to her comic book.

His heart raced.

At school that morning, he was unable to concentrate. He ran the scenarios over and over again in his head. Was it a coworker? An old friend? Something more?

It was probably innocent, he thought.

Probably.

At his locker after first period, he felt a hand on his shoulder and jumped.

"Sheesh, you're jumpy today," his girlfriend Cassie said, raising both arms as if under arrest. She had dark, chocolate-colored skin and short dark hair that spiked its ends. She was smiling at him. It seemed she liked him today.

"Sorry," he said. "Stuff going on. With the family."

"Oh," she said, her shoulders arching up. "Well . . ."

"It's nothing," he said. "Sorry. What's up with you?"

"Just wanted to see you," she said, smiling at him. "Did

you get your mid-term grade for physics? I had the highest score in econ."

"Good for you." He tried to smile. She would probably have the highest score in all her classes. If not, she might call him, that night, to run frantically through the test, trying to determine exactly where it had all gone wrong (or where the teacher had messed up in grading). "I got an A-."

"That's great, Matt," she said, beaming at him. It was great, or fine anyway, but something about the way she said it made him feel inadequate. If she had been the one with the A-, it wouldn't have been "great."

"I guess," he said.

"It *is* great," she said, cupping her hands around his cheeks. "You're brilliant, I'm brilliant; we're going to go off to college, then take over the world."

Today, she said that. Tomorrow, she would be distant and moody, pulling away when he tried to touch her, telling him she didn't want to talk about it, looking at him with those glaring, pinched eyes.

He didn't really blame her.

His mother was being charged with vehicular manslaughter. Driving with a blood alcohol level of 0.09, getting into an accident resulting in the death of a girl. In the death of Chloe, Cassie's best friend.

Still.

He wasn't the one driving.

Cassie leaned forward and kissed him, her tongue wrapping around his. She must have been pumped about the grade —she leaned her body deeply into his, pressing against him. He let his hands drift slowly down her back—slowly, achingly —but when they got to her butt, she put a hand on his chest and pushed him back.

"C'mon, Cass, I wasn't doing anything."

"I can't, Matt. You know I can't."

That was the other thing with Cassie. The whole virgin thing.

"What, kiss your boyfriend?"

She narrowed her dark eyes. "Don't start," she said. Then, "I'm going to be late for class."

She turned then, and he watched her overstuffed backpack bounce against the back of her skin-tight t-shirt as she vanished into the crowd. If he'd had his camera on him, he would have snapped a picture.

The bell rang. He was late.

He waited a few moments to get back in control. Then he just stood there.

After a minute, he shoved his entire backpack into the locker. Spun the combination lock.

Then went to find Jade.

His cousin was supposed to be in English class, but when he peeked in the window of the room, her usual seat in the back was empty. He headed to the art room and found her sitting on a side table beside her friend, chewing gum and gesturing wildly. Ms. Harris, the art teacher, was known for welcoming drop-ins, whom she supposedly assumed were on their lunch hour. At nine in the morning.

"Aren't you supposed to be in class?" he asked.

"I am in class," she said with a grin, kicking her combat-boot-clad feet back and forth.

"You know what I mean," he said.

"And where are you supposed to be?"

He grinned back. "In class."

"What's up, Matty?" she asked.

He looked around, made sure Ms. Harris was out of earshot. "I need to get out of here," he said.

Jade's barbell-clad eyebrow danced upward. A smile slowly spread across her face. "Sorry, Lace, my honor roll cousin is a bad influence on me," she said, hopping off the table. "I'll meet you after school?"

"Sure," her friend said. "Have fun being corrupted."

"And I was so innocent and pure."

They giggled.

Jade led him through some weird exit in the back of the auxiliary art room. Once they had safely exited the school, Jade turned on him. "What the hell is going on?"

"I thought you liked skipping school."

"I don't know that I'd say I *like* it," she said, stomping through the snow toward his car. "I mean, it beats *going* to school . . ."

He chuckled.

"Seriously, why are you skipping?"

"I have stuff I need to work out," he said, opening the driver's side door and sliding in. "I couldn't pay attention in there. And I wanted someone to talk to."

"And Little Miss Perfect didn't want to skip with you?"

He rolled his eyes and eased out of the parking space. "Well, it has to do with my family, so I don't think she wants to hear about it."

"You know what your problem is, Matt?" Jade asked. She rolled down the window and lit a cigarette. Held it to her lips with two fingers. Inhaled.

"No, but I'm sure you're going to tell me." Matt watched as the smoke she blew out blended into the gray of the sky. His fingers twitched, but his camera had been left behind, inside his locker. And besides that, he was driving.

He turned his eyes to the road in front of them. The same road, the same spot, where everything had gone off the rails.

He couldn't wait to be done with this place.

"Your problem," she said, "is that you don't push anything. Your parents stop talking to each other, you do nothing; your mom wants to move out, you say OK; your girlfriend refuses to talk about anything, you let her."

"You can't force someone to talk," he said.

"Bull," she said. She took another drag on her cigarette. "You're just afraid of what she'll say."

Cold air blew in through the window as she exhaled.

"Where are we going?" he asked.

"You're so bad at this," she said. "Even when you're not in school, you have to have a plan. A destination." She took another drag on the cigarette. "We could hit the park."

"The park? It's January."

"Yes, Matty, the park does still exist in the winter. I know it may be hard to believe . . ."

"What about your house?"

"Kicked out."

Of course she was. He drummed his fingers on the steering wheel.

"What about my house?"

"No," she said simply.

So he drove to the park.

When they got there, Jade took off for the playground in a mad sprint. Matt zipped his coat tightly and pulled on his thickest gloves, then walked slowly behind.

He found her in the top tower of the wooden structure, leaning out of the cutout window, white smoke wafting up from the end of her cigarette.

"See?" she said. "Shelter. And we can huddle around my cigarette for warmth."

He let out a sigh, then climbed up and sat down beside her.

"So, what's up?" she asked. She was perched on a bench, cigarette between two fingers in fingerless gloves. Fishnets were visible beneath the rips in her jeans.

He shrugged. "Aren't you cold?"

"Eskimos don't get cold," she said cryptically. "So, what's

up? Mr. Honor Society, skipping class. First time ever, unless you're skipping with someone I don't know."

"No, you're the only degenerate I know," he said, shivering.

She stuck out her lower lip. "I feel sad for you. We degenerates make the best company."

He smiled wanly.

"Matty?" She looked at him with arched eyebrows. Reached out to shove his shoulder. "C'mon, what's going on?"

"I found something," he said finally. He ran a hand across his mouth. "On my dad's phone. It's probably nothing."

"Ooh, is it porn?"

He narrowed his eyes at her.

"Sorry," she said, twirling a red-streaked ponytail through her fingers. "What was it?"

"Just these texts. From this woman. It's probably just a friend or something."

Jade leaned forward, elbows resting on her knees. "What did they say?" Smoke from her cigarette drifted toward the roof of the structure.

His teeth chattered. "Just, *Had fun last night. Let's do it again.* Like I said, though, it's probably nothing." He drummed his gloved fingers against the floor.

Jade took a long drag on her cigarette. "I never would have thought Uncle Sam would be the type," she mused. "Then again, I never would have thought Aunt Amanda would get arrested for a DUI manslaughter thing, so—"

"Don't," he said. "Like I said, it's probably nothing."

"It's clearly bothering you." She stubbed out her cigarette and lit a fresh one. Took a drag.

"Well, everything's bothering me," he said. "My family is falling apart." He wiggled his toes to keep them from turning to ice. "My girlfriend, the one person I'm supposed to be able to talk to about all of this, my fucking *rock*, blames me for all of this.

She can barely stand to look at me some days. Other days, she loves me. But not if I talk about this. Not *ever* if I talk about this. I just want everything to go back the way it was. I have nothing.

"There was a plan," he continued. "Everyone had a plan and an order and a way it was supposed to be. And it worked. We were all happy. My family. Me and Cassie. And then everything got screwed to hell. I woke up in some alternate reality. Sometimes I don't even feel real anymore. Everything's foggy. Like I'm just drifting through space, and this is all just some kind of dream, you know?"

She turned to look at him. "What are you on?" she asked. "And can I get some?"

"Cute," he said.

"You know what your problem is, Matty?" she asked, taking another drag on her cigarette. "Your life was too bloody perfect. All along. Everyone was happy. Something bad happened, and no one knew what to do."

"Not like your life?"

"I can handle it," she said, her brown eyes boring into his.

"Right," he said. "Tell me that again after your mom cuts off your credit card."

Jade shook her head and gave him the finger. "Don't talk to me," she said. "You have a friggin' place to sleep every night."

"Jade, you have a hundred places to sleep at night," he told her. "I'm sure you could go home if you really wanted to. And there's always my place."

She glared at him, then stubbed out her cigarette and rose. She leaned backward through the cut-out window in the wall, tilting, tilting, daring gravity to drag her to the earth.

"Stop that," he said.

"Please," he added when she didn't respond.

Jade leaned back in. Lit a fresh cigarette.

"She moved out," he reminded her. "Or are you cutting all of us off?"

"It's just too weird. Everything there just reminds me . . . of how it used to be, and, well . . ." Jade shrugged and looked away.

We miss you, he thought.

"I don't blame your mom anymore," she said.

Tell her that, he thought.

"It's never coming back, Matty," she said. She rolled a pigtail around her exposed finger. "I always thought your family was perfect, but it never really was, was it?"

He said nothing. He shifted his numb feet.

"Your problem is you don't want to accept it. Your mom has moved out and might go to jail. Your dad is probably sleeping with someone else. I know you don't want to accept it, but—"

"I have a lot of problems," he observed. He ripped off his gloves and blew on his fists for warmth. He could barely feel his toes.

She grinned widely. "Not as many as me."

He snorted. "Fuck," he said. "What am I going to do?"

She inhaled deeply from her cigarette. "You could try asking him."

"No," he said, shaking his head. "I can't do that. It's probably nothing."

"Your family is so messed up," she said, blowing one, two, three rings of smoke at him. "I mean, don't get me wrong, you guys were nice, and most of the time you were pretty happy, but you never talk about anything even moderately unpleasant. Sure, it worked for a while, but now . . . and you and Cassie are doing the same damn thing. It's like one of those learned behaviors or something. A vicious spiral."

"It's a vicious cycle," he corrected, still blowing on his hands.

"Yes, Mr. Grammar Police." She gave him the finger, then took another hit of her cigarette.

"Can I try?" he asked.

"Smoking?"

"Yeah."

"Matty, of all my stupid habits to pick up . . ." She shook her head. "You don't even get high and you do get cancer."

"Then why do you smoke?"

She ground her cigarette butt against the wall of the tower and then flung it out the window to the snow below. "I'm addicted. I mean, it started as a *fuck you* to my mom, but now I'm hooked."

She pulled her pack and lighter out of her pocket. Smacked it hard against her knee. Three times. Then took out a fresh cigarette and lit up.

He put out his hand, fingers scissored apart.

She shrugged and passed him the cigarette.

He brought it to his lips and sucked in.

He coughed and sputtered. Banged on his chest with his fist.

Passed the cigarette back to Jade and tried to catch his breath.

"Was it everything you thought it would be?" she asked, smile half-cocked.

"Yes," he said, meeting her gaze.

She shook her head, then grinned.

"Look," she said after a moment. "You can't just sit on this. It's going to eat you alive, I swear to God it will. You need proof, go hack his email or follow him or something. But you can't just push this down, pretend it never happened. It will fucking destroy you."

He licked his lips. They were chapping in the cold, dry air. "OK," he said finally.

She grinned widely at him, smoke spilling from between her teeth.

"That's disgusting," he said. "You know you're getting emphysema, right? And it's not pleasant. You should see what some of those lungs look like—"

"That's the cousin I know and love," she said. She stubbed out the cigarette and tossed it out the window. "Always so responsible."

"Do you think maybe that's my problem?" he asked.

"Oh, absolutely. And, hey, admitting you have a problem is the first step."

He shook his head, then rose. "I can't stay here," he said. "It's too cold."

Jade shrugged. "Want to drive around, then?"

"Sure."

"So what's your plan?" Jade asked once they were back in the relative warmth of his car. "With your dad?"

"I have no idea," he said.

"Do you know who it is?" she asked, jamming her phone onto his charger. "Like, is it someone he works with?"

"All I know is it's someone named Susanna," he said.

"No fucking way." Jade's head jerked up, away from the phone. "You don't think it's—"

"Who?" he asked. He felt his eyebrows furrow.

"Lacey's mom. The new guidance counselor. Ms. Simms? Her name's Susanna."

"Susanna's a common name." He eased onto a side street. Tried to picture the guidance counselor in his head. And then he could, and other images swam in, images of the two of them, reaching toward each other . . . and he had to shake his head to clear it.

"She just got divorced," Jade offered. "Nasty story. But I'm not one to start rumors or anything."

"Then don't," he said, irritated.

"OK, Matty, chill. I'm not the one who created this situation. I could be wrong. Just, you know, something to check out."

"Sure," he muttered.

"So I'm thinking of getting a tattoo," she said suddenly. "A big *FU* on my forehead. In, like, university letterhead. I think it would look awesome."

He blinked at her, then turned back to the road. "Seriously?"

"Well, maybe on my shoulder," she amended. "But I definitely want it."

"And are you still going to want it when you're forty?" he asked.

"Probably not." She grinned. "But I want it now."

He shook his head and tried not to smile.

That evening, before he even had time to process exactly what he had promised Jade, his father poked his head through the doorway to the basement. "I'm going out for coffee," he said. "One of my colleagues. I'll be back in a couple of hours. Can you make sure Jenna eats something?"

"Sure," he said.

He waited.

He thought about just letting it go. Ordering pizza, dragging Jenna out of her room. Watching something on cable. A nice night, inside, warm.

He went upstairs. He could hear his father's footsteps in the garage. He rushed out the front door without even bothering to grab a coat, then darted down the snow-covered walk. His car was parked in front of the house. He unlocked it as the garage door was opening. He slid inside and hunched down as he watched his father's taillights back slowly down the driveway.

Then he started the car and followed.

They didn't go far. Just a few miles, just into town. His father worked at the university two towns over.

Still, it was possible a colleague lived in the area. Or was driving out here to meet him.

His father parked behind the café, then got out of his car and headed for the rear entrance. So at least that much was true. Matt drove past, then circled back and parked.

He debated what to do. The place was small. No way he could walk in without them noticing. Then he looked at his passenger seat and noticed Jenna's hoodie. His hoodie, really, which she had repurposed last year. She had taken it off on the drive home from school, complaining that there must be something wrong with the car.

"It's burning up in here," she'd said. "And it's like, freezing outside. Plus, I smell smoke. I'm telling you, this car is about to go nuclear or something."

He slipped on the black sweatshirt, pulling the hood down so that it partially obstructed his vision.

He got out of the car and walked around to the front of the restaurant, shivering beneath the thin sweatshirt. Jammed his fists into his pockets and walked slowly past the front window, glancing up every so often. His father sat alone at a table, newspaper spread before him.

Matt froze, held his breath.

And then he saw a woman, out on the sidewalk with him. Walking past him without a glance. Going inside, slipping off her coat. Looking over toward his father. Waving.

A woman.

His guidance counselor.

Susanna.

He wanted to call Cassie. But the old Cassie, from back before. The one who loved his family, the one who would have been just as crushed as him. The one who would have held him and kissed him and maybe let him feel her up, just this once.

Not the ice queen, who would shut him down before he even opened his mouth.

. . .

He went home. What else was there to do? He ordered pizza and called Jenna down for dinner.

"Dad's got a meeting or something," he told her.

She shrugged. "Can I eat in my room?"

"Sure."

He thought about the night, just before Christmas, that their mother had told them she was leaving. He'd stormed out of the house, seeking comfort, first from Cassie, who just didn't want to talk about it, and then from Jade, who was nice enough not to remind him that she had told him to grow a pair and call them on their shit months ago.

And then he had come home and found Jenna sitting on his basement sofa, wrapped in a blanket, waiting.

"I want Mom back," she'd said. Her lower lip wavered. "I want everything back." She hadn't said it was all his fault. For blaming their mother, for making her feel unwelcome. She also hadn't said that it was all his fault that there was even an accident. How he was supposed to be her ride, but had kept putting her off, ignoring her increasingly frustrated texts, wanting to spend more time in the school darkroom.

"I know," he'd said. "I'm sorry. Maybe they'll work it out."

And she had looked up at him and said one small thing: "I don't want to be alone right now."

And so they had sat there all night, on his half-falling-apart sofa, channel surfing, dozing off, and mostly just sighing.

Waiting to wake up.

Tonight, he waited alone.

. . .

When his father came in, Matt was sitting at the dining room table, a plate of cold pizza in front of him.

"Save any pizza?" his father asked.

Matt stared.

Then, quietly, he said, "Are you sleeping with her?"

His father looked at him like he'd seen a ghost. Blinked. Set down his keys on the counter with a clink. Slowly took off his coat, then laid it down on top of his keys.

Matt wondered for a moment if he had heard. The heat clicked on and a blast of warm air burst out from the vent.

"No," his father said at last. "How did you—"

"Text message this morning," Matt said. "You were in your office or something."

"Shit." He ran a hand through his hair, then came and sat down at the table across from Matt. "We were just friends," he said. "That was it. Just somebody to talk to."

"*Were?*"

His father rested two fingers across his lips. Took a long breath. "When your mother left . . . She'd probably tell you it was because of her. Because of Susanna. She saw some texts. But we were just friends, I swear. I swear, Matt, I would never do anything to mess up this family. You kids—"

Matt put a hand up to stop him. So many questions swirled in his head.

"You said you *were* just friends. But now?"

His father closed his eyes and massaged his forehead with two fingers. "It's complicated. We haven't really talked about it, Susanna and I. We're . . . spending time together. If your mother hadn't left . . . I would never cheat on her. And we're not sleeping together, Susanna and I."

Matt pressed his lips together. "Not yet," he said, more a question than a statement.

"I'm not going to lie to you, Matt. Down the line, in the future—"

Matt put his hand up again. "What about Mom?" he asked.

His father pushed up his glasses and rubbed his eyes. "I'm sorry," he said. "We tried. I . . . It just wasn't working. We should have been more upfront with you kids. We should have told you . . . but I didn't want to hurt you any more than was necessary . . . I figured with time, you would come to accept it . . . I figured—"

"You didn't try." Matt stood. He felt his blood rushing to his face. "You barely spoke to her. How the hell is that trying?"

His father looked up at him, met his eyes. "You're right. We've never been good, your mother and I, we've never been good at fighting. I spent a lot of time, in my head, trying to figure out what to say to her, or what I wanted to say to her, how to say it right . . . I couldn't get there. She needed me to say it was OK, that it didn't change anything, but—"

"Bullshit!" Matt spat at him. "That is fucking bullshit! She needed you to say you still loved her. That you would work on it. That you would try. That you would fight, *anything*. We never even heard you two fight. Never heard you yelling at each other. You don't just throw everything away without a fight!"

"We fought," his father said quietly. "In our own way. After the accident, every time she looked at me, we had a little fight in my head. And I couldn't come up with anything to say that wouldn't just make things worse. So I didn't say anything. And then she started drinking, and that was another fight, every night. She wanted something from me, and I wanted something from her. She hated that I didn't talk to her. I didn't know what to say. It wasn't her fault, not really. She started something, but it could have been anything, really. We just couldn't, we just couldn't handle it. In the end, we were both just tired of fighting. Or not fighting."

Matt said nothing then. Just turned and walked toward the door.

"Where are you going?" he heard his father ask half-heartedly.

Matt ignored him.

For the second time, he went out into the night without a coat. He got into his car and drove.

The motel was at the far end of town, just past the highway, its peeling flint-gray paint barely visible beneath a single overhead light.

He banged on the door.

There was no answer.

He banged again, his fist becoming heavier as it froze.

Then he heard the locks click—one, two, three—and the door opened.

His mother stood, staring at him, her face slack, looking like she hadn't showered in days, her hair more dirty than blond.

"Matt!" she said, surprised. The sides of her lips curled up. As of late, he'd hated the way she did that, as if expecting him to just forgive her. Now, though, it just made him sad.

"What's wrong?" she asked as he stepped into the room, light spilling onto his features.

"You need to come home," he said. He left the door open behind him. Cold blasted against his back.

"Is everything OK? Jenna? Your father?" Her hand was at her mouth.

"No one's hurt," he said. "You need to come home."

"Close the door, please," she said.

"You need to come home," he repeated, shifting from foot to foot. "Get your things. I'll drive you."

"Matt." She reached up and touched his face. "Sweetie, what's going on?"

He sighed. Pushed the door closed behind him. "If you don't come home soon," he said, "there won't be anything left for you to come home to."

He surveyed the room. Normally he didn't go inside. Just dropped Jenna off, or picked his mother up for one appointment or another. He let her buy him Taco Bell a couple of times when she insisted on visiting. Now, he looked around. Two sagging beds, a microwave, a trashcan stuffed full of pizza boxes. A dresser, the faux wood beginning to peel.

His mother shook her head slowly. She stepped back and sank down onto the unmade bed. "I'm sorry," she said. "I don't know how to fix it. I can't go back in time, and I can't change the way other people feel."

"He's not sleeping with her," Matt said quickly. "Yet. Come home before he does. Come home now. I know it sucks right now, but it will get better. Dad knows it wasn't really your fault; it wasn't even about that. He knows what he's doing isn't right. You guys just need to figure out how to talk to each other and everything will be OK. Just come home, please."

He didn't know what else to say.

"Oh, Matt," she said, face in her hands. "I am so sorry, baby. I messed everything up. There was a brake, I meant to hit the brake. My foot slipped, I got confused . . . I hit the gas. I never saw their car, I swear I didn't, but I hit the gas."

He walked over, rested a hand on her shoulder. "It's OK," he said. "It was an accident."

Her shoulders shook. "A girl died," she said. "She had a mother, she had friends, she was alive. And now she's dead. She's dead."

"Mom." He leaned closer. Then he took a step back. "Are you drunk?"

She wiped her eyes and looked up at him. "I just had a couple of glasses of wine," she said.

"Seriously," he said. He ran his fingers through his hair,

pulling at the roots. "After everything, this is what you're doing?"

"I'm sorry," she said. "I wasn't expecting you. I wasn't hurting anyone. I—"

"You weren't hurting anyone? What about me and Jenna? All we want is our family back, and you're sitting here drowning it all in cheap wine."

"Matt," she said, her voice a whimper. She stood and walked toward him. "Sweetie, it was already over. And I'm sorry, I am so sorry. I don't expect you to understand. It wasn't over because I drank. It wasn't over because I left. I drank because it was over and I left because it was over."

"You didn't fight!" He stabbed his finger in her direction, face flushing. "You didn't fight for it. You didn't scream at each other and go to therapy and whatever the hell else you're supposed to do. It got hard and you just couldn't handle it. Neither of you."

"I'm sorry," she said again, tears running down her cheeks.

"Don't be sorry," he said. "Fix it. Stop drinking, right now. Clean yourself up. Come home. *Try*. Put up with all the pain and all the misery. I don't care if you feel like crap all the time. I don't care how hard it is. Just try, goddamn it!"

"I can't," she said. She sunk back into the bed and pulled on her unkempt hair. "I can't be around him, all the stares, all the silence. Your father and I never really forgive each other, you know that?"

He licked his lips. He could hear his heart thudding in his ears.

"Because you never talk about it!"

"I don't know how," she said. Tears streaked her cheeks. "We've been filling that box for twenty years, Matt. Twenty years of resentments, twenty years of things we didn't say."

"You can change!"

"I'm tired." She shook her head. "I'm so tired of fighting with him. I just need his voice out of my head. I'm so sorry,

Matt. I'll make things better with you and Jenna. I will. We can still be a family, the three of us."

There was a vision in his head. All four of them, in the kitchen, eating freshly made waffles with all the toppings. Laughing, talking, Jenna reaching over with her spoon to steal his whipped cream.

He closed his eyes and let it fade.

"You can quit drinking," he finally said, sitting down on the other bed. "It would be something."

"I'm sorry," she said. She covered her face with her hands. He could see that she had been chewing on her nails. Her shoulders shook. "Before, I could have. You have to understand that. It was backward. It was just for fun before. Just a little bit, though obviously a bit too much that day. But I didn't think about it, before. Sometimes I drank, sometimes I didn't. It wasn't anything.

"Now, I close my eyes and I see their faces, her face, the blood, you kids, your father, all of it, playing over and over and over again. Then I think about her mother, and what I would feel if it was me, if something had happened to one of my babies . . . and I just need to throw a blanket over the whole thing. I just need to be safe, inside my head, for just a little while. The wine turns down the volume, makes everything warm and safe for a while. I should quit, I know," she held up her hand, "but tell me, Matt, what do I gain if I do?"

He stared at her, his fingers resting across his lips.

"My respect," he whispered.

"Oh, Matt," she said, and she sobbed harder.

"It's OK, Mom," he said finally. "It's OK." He rose, hugged her shaking head.

"I'm so sorry," she said.

"I know," he said.

After he left, he drove aimlessly.

He wished he could go back to that day. In the darkroom. Jenna's texts. He wished he had responded, at least, with "*just a minute*." Anything to keep her from calling for another ride. But at the time, he had wanted her to get another ride. Why should he be burdened with his little sister's needs? Why should he rearrange his schedule so she could lay around doing nothing at home instead of at school?

By the time he had emerged from the darkness, he could hear sirens in the distance.

He wished, too, that he had run up and found Cassie. Insisted on riding in the ambulance with her.

Instead, he had driven Jenna to the hospital to get her checked out while their mother was getting booked.

He should have looked for Cassie while he was there, but he hadn't. He didn't know how bad it was. He thought they would be fine. He thought the biggest drama in his life was his own.

He should have gone to the funeral, but he hadn't wanted people staring at him.

He should have talked to her, should have told her everything, even the things she didn't want to hear.

He turned left, then right.

And headed over to Cassie's.

6

TRUTH OR SOMETHING LIKE IT

In March, my dad and the guidance counselor decide I should see a shrink.

I picture someone with a beard and glasses, but instead I get a short guy with a goatee. He looks like a leprechaun. He sits across from me and strokes his goatee. I look around and can't find a clock. I don't want to be rude.

I look at my watch. Forty-eight minutes to go.

SHRINK (holding up his hand in a half-wave): Hello, Jenna. I'm Jeremy.

I think it's weird to call adults by their first names.

ME (hands folded in my lap): Hi.

SHRINK: So what brings you in?

ME (shrugging):

He knows what brings me in. I'm sure they filled him in when they made the appointment. What am I supposed to say? "My mom is probably maybe going to jail because she had a car accident and someone died. My parents are maybe getting a divorce because she had margaritas at lunch."

SHRINK (smiling for unknown reasons): Not very talkative?

I swear, if he says, "Cat got your tongue?" I'm bolting for the restroom and never coming back. I am not some stupid little kid. I am in high school now, and I know how things work.

ME: They made me come.

SHRINK (hand on chin, the classic pose): Well, do this one time for them, and then you can decide if you want to come back.

ME: OK.

SHRINK (stroking goatee): So who made you come here?

ME: My dad and the guidance counselor.

My dad and the woman he's probably sleeping with.

————

When I wake up one night in February and cannot fall back to sleep, I go down the two flights of stairs to my brother's basement. His kingdom. All black and green paint, aluminum-foil-wrapped pipes.

I sit on the couch that used to be our couch, before my mom decided she wanted a microfiber one. A baby blue microfiber one that meant she had to repaint the living room in blue-gray.

She is staying at a motel now and doesn't have a couch. Every time I go upstairs to sit on our couch, I think about helping her paint the living room, and then I get sad.

I don't spend much time on the main floor anymore.

I sit on the old couch and I wait.

My brother comes in at five in the morning.

ME (arms folded): Where were you?

MATT: What are you, Mom?

ME:

MATT: I was out for a run.

Matt is good at running. And photography. And guitar. And school. And girls. And life.

ME:

MATT (kicking off his shoes): What are you doing waiting up?

ME: Dad's not home either.

MATT: Shit.

ME:

MATT (not looking at me): You need to get over your whole fantasy, Jenna.

ME (picking at the hole in my socks):

MATT (looking up): I'm sorry; I'm not trying to be a jerk.

ME: What fantasy?

MATT: Mom and Dad. Working it out, getting back together. Something. It's not going to happen. It sucks, but . . . the sooner you let it go, the sooner you can move on with things.

ME:

MATT (under his breath): I guess Dad's sleeping with Susanna now.

ME: What? Who?

MATT: Ms. Simms. The guidance counselor. The new one, who was all *concerned* after the accident. Not the old one with the skin condition.

ME:

Matt comes over and pats my head, like I'm some sort of dog.

MATT: They didn't get together until after Mom left.

ME (back arching): What makes you think they're together?

MATT: He told me, more or less. They were just friends. Nothing happened until after Mom moved out.

ME: What makes you think something happened?

MATT (waving an arm out): He was out all night.

ME: It could be something else. They could just be friends.

Matt's back is to me; he is digging through a drawer looking for something.

MATT: No, I talked to Dad about it. They . . . after Mom left . . . they got to be more than friends.

ME:

MATT (over his shoulder): It sucks, I know. Believe me, if I could do something about it . . .

ME: I can't believe you talked to him about that.

Matt shrugs.

ME: Is that why you think you can get away with staying out all night?

MATT: That, and my sister's got my back.

He winks at me.

ME: Where were you?

MATT: Where do you think? Cassie's.

He comes back to the couch with a bag of peanut butter M&Ms. He waves the bag in my direction, but I shake my head.

ME: What if her dad has a gun?

MATT (tossing an M&M into his mouth): He doesn't have a gun.

ME:

MATT:

ME: Can you maybe not stay out when Dad stays out? I got up at three in the morning and everyone was gone. For a second I wondered if I had slipped into one of those internet conspiracy parallel dimensions or something . . .

MATT: I'll talk to Dad.

ME (grabbing his arm): Don't! Please, Matt.

MATT: Fine, whatever. I'll check to make sure his car's in the garage before I go out.

ME: Thanks.

I take a few M&Ms.

MATT: Are you pissed at Dad?

ME:

MATT: Mom gave up too, you know.

ME:

MATT (leaning his head back against the couch): I know, it sucks.

———

SHRINK (legs crossed): So what happened the day of the accident?

ME (pulling on my lower lip with my fingernails): My mom was driving past an intersection. A two-way stop—the other side was supposed to stop, not us. I was looking out the window at the house on the corner—it has all this peeling paint and a really nice Mustang in the driveway and I always wonder who lives there—and all of a sudden this car sped in front of us and we couldn't stop in time. We weren't speeding or anything, I mean, we had just gotten out of the parking lot, but one of the girls in the other car died anyway. She wasn't wearing a seat belt. Their car was really flimsy and just kind of collapsed. I think it was foreign.

SHRINK: And your mother had been drinking?

ME (looking up at the ceiling): Well, maybe a drink or two at lunch. She wasn't supposed to pick me up, but Matt was taking forever developing some photos or something, so I called her and she came to get me. She was barely over the limit. Under the limit, according to the old law. It was just bad timing. I mean, all around, obviously. But since the other driver pulled in front of us, it shouldn't matter that she just was a hair over the limit.

SHRINK: You've studied this a lot.

ME (shrugging):

———

COP 1: So, just tell me what happened. What you remember. If you don't remember anything, that's OK too.

ME: I don't know.

COP 2: That's OK, just take your time.

The room is probably the same one where they interrogate suspects. I wonder if they interrogated my mother. If it's anything like it is on TV, I want to kill them.

The room is dark and windowless and the chairs are not comfortable. There is a camera in the corner. So they cannot hurt me. So I cannot lie and say they hurt me. So I cannot lie and say, "I never said that."

ME (blinking): I never saw the car.

COP 1: That's fine.

ME: I mean, I was looking out my window and it came so quickly. They came from my side, didn't they? One second I was looking up the street and at this house on the corner. It's got all of this peeling paint, but sometimes there's a nice car in the driveway. Then there was the car. Right in front of us. A lot of noise. Brakes, she slammed her brakes.

COP 2: The other driver?

ME: No, my mom.

They glance at each other.

COPS:

ME (glaring at them): I know she slammed her brakes because I jerked forward. I dropped my head and that's when I hit it. On the dashboard. Then we hit the car.

COP 1: Do you remember anything else?

ME (eyes wide, trying to talk as slowly as possible so as not to seem hysterical): My mom looked before she turned. She stopped and she looked and everything. They weren't there. They just came flying out of nowhere.

————

SHRINK: So your mother was not at fault?

ME (leaning forward): No, of course not. Don't try to—

SHRINK (backing, ever so slightly, into his chair): I'm not questioning it. I'm on your side.

ME:

———

MOM: So I know this place isn't very nice . . .

I am lying on the spare bed in her sparse room in the 1970s-era motel. She should get an apartment, but she can't commit to a lease. She might be in jail in a few months.

She doesn't have a couch. Her TV only gets twenty channels. Her "kitchen" is a microwave and a mini-fridge. There are empty pizza boxes in the trash. Not even McDonald's, just to break things up. They don't deliver. And she can't drive.

ME: It's fine. It's kind of cool. I mean, it has a pool.

MOM (scrunching her nose up): I don't think I want you going in that pool.

ME: Well, obviously not now. It's the middle of winter.

MOM: In a few months, once the court case is done—then, then I can make a better plan. Get a job, have some income. Find a nice place to rent.

ME (twisting a shoelace around my finger): Maybe you could come back home.

MOM:

ME (running my tongue against my teeth until it hurts): A townhouse could be nice.

MOM: One of those tall ones, with the loft areas up top.

ME (plastering a smile): That would be cool.

MOM: I miss you.

ME (looking everywhere but at her): I miss you too.

MOM: Soon. A couple of months. They'll settle this thing.

ME: Yeah, it'll fly by.

MOM: I'm so sorry.

ME: It's fine. It wasn't your fault.

MOM (a flash of a tired smile): Thanks.

ME:

MOM (twisting a napkin between her fingers): That thing, with the police. You said she just pulled right out of nowhere?

ME: Yes.

MOM: My attorney thinks . . . it would be very helpful . . . if you could say that . . . at the trial . . .

ME (shrugging): OK.

MOM: It might be kind of hard.

ME (eyebrows scrunching together): Why would it be hard? It's the truth. I want to talk to them. I want to help.

MOM (twisting her unkempt hair): I don't know if your dad will want you to . . . he doesn't want you pulled into all of this . . . he doesn't want me doing more damage.

ME (looking at her): You didn't do any damage, Mom.

MOM (face about to break): You're so sweet.

ME: Don't worry about Dad. It would do a lot more damage to me if I don't get to do this.

———

SHRINK: How will you feel if your mother goes to jail?

ME (arms folded): She's not going to jail.

SHRINK: But, just for a thought exercise . . .

ME: She's not going to jail.

SHRINK:

ME: Why do you ask these questions? You obviously know the answer. You just want me to say it.

SHRINK: It can be helpful for you to verbalize what you feel. And each person's experience is different. I'd like to know more about what aspect would be the most difficult for you.

ME: She's not going to jail.

———

Vivien is braiding a strip of my hair. She is girlier than I am. Which is to say she does things like braid hair and paint nails and put on makeup. No skirts, though, and nothing pink. She is not that girly. She's a short Asian girl with a blunt haircut and bangs. She has really cute square-rimmed glasses and wears Star Trek *and* Mathletes *t-shirts. She is really smart.*

ME (trying to keep my head still for Vivien): What if she goes to jail?

VIVIEN (cocking her head to the side and looking me up and down): You'll be OK.

ME: I'll be all alone. My house gets so quiet. Matt is always doing something or over at Cassie's. My dad's grading papers or working on his book. Or with her. I can turn the TV up as loud as it goes and it's still too quiet.

VIVIEN (nodding): But you're strong. You'll be OK. It won't be easy, but you'll survive. And you'll have one of those really interesting life stories that you can write a novel about or something.

I want to tell her she's wrong, that I am not strong, but she runs a hand down my arm. It's warm and strong and I want to be that way too.

VIVIEN: And you won't really be alone. I'm just a text away.

ME (smiling): How after-school special of you.

VIVIEN: I love a good after-school special.

Vivien and I never used to be friends. Science partners, sure. I never thought she really liked me, because I just kind of let her do most of the work on our projects. But neither one of us really had any friends, and after the accident, while everyone else was avoiding me, or glaring at me or worse, she was nice. Really nice. Like, "Come, sit with me," in the cafeteria. And, "Do you want to come over after school?" when she found me sitting in the hall, waiting for my brother to give me a ride home.

ME (closing my eyes): What if she does go to jail? What is she going to do there? What if they hurt her?

VIVIEN (touching my arm again): She'll go to some Martha Stewart place. Make Christmas ornaments out of popsicle sticks and do other lame crafts. It'll be like camp.

ME: Except you can't leave.

VIVIEN (squeezing my arm): But you can visit.

ME: It won't be the same.

VIVIEN: No.

ME: What if she doesn't get out until I'm out of high school? Then it's all over; she's missed everything.

VIVIEN: She'll have missed the crappy years. According to my mom, most of us are little bitches in high school.

ME: Your mom didn't really say that.

VIVIEN: Oh, yes she did. My mom can be really mouthy when she wants to be.

She finishes with my braid and pushes me toward the mirror.

VIVIEN: What do you think?

With my long red hair, it makes me look like someone out of the Renaissance Fair. Girlier than I would normally look.

ME (smiling): I love it.

Vivien rests an arm on my shoulder and I study her reflection in the mirror behind me. She is smiling.

———

SHRINK: OK, you're not ready to talk about the possibility of your mother going to jail.

ME (arms folded):

SHRINK: She's not living at home now, is that correct?

ME: Yes.

SHRINK: That must be a big change for you. How was it before, when she lived at home?

ME: It was nice, obviously.

———

MATT (palms flat against the kitchen counter): So, how would you solve poverty in America?

ME (shrugging): I don't know, give everyone a million dollars.

MATT: I mean, realistically. You can't just pull a few trillion dollars out of your ass.

DAD (over his shoulder from the fridge): The Fed can.

MATT: Yeah, well, then you have inflation and a million dollars isn't worth the paper it's printed on.

MOM: But everyone has it.

MATT (gesturing wildly): Then you're talking communism, and we know that doesn't work.

MOM (setting down her coffee mug): OK, Matt, how would you solve things?

MATT: I don't think there is a solution. The whole system is broken and no one in Washington can get their head out of their ass long enough to fix things.

DAD (looking at Mom): So young to be so cynical.

MOM (to Matt): At least your sister tried to come up with a plan.

ME: It'd be nice to have a million dollars.

MOM: I would get one of those houses with the secret passages. And a theater.

ME: We could get the whole place wired with fiber optic cable.

MATT: You're missing the point. If everyone had a million dollars, a house like that would cost two million.

ME: Mom can have my million.

MOM (winking at me): Aw, thanks.

MATT: Well, it would cost, like, twenty million.

ME: You can't just keep raising the price.

MATT (throwing his arms up): That's what happens in an inflationary economy!

MOM: I think I want the house to have two living rooms.

One blue, one mauve. Just so I can say, "Oh, it's in my *other* living room."

ME: Plus, a rec room and a den and a family room.

MOM: Maybe a solarium.

MATT: Are you trying to drive me crazy?

DAD: By jove, I think you've finally cracked their code.

MATT: Here I am, trying to have a conversation about important things . . .

———

SHRINK: Did your parents ever fight?

ME: No.

ME (biting my lip): They didn't fight.

———

DAD: What do you want for breakfast?

ME: Waffles.

MATT: Coffee.

MOM:

DAD: Doing anything cool in school today?

ME: Dad, it's school.

MATT: There's a sit-in to protest the quality of food in the cafeteria.

ME: So, what, everyone sits at their tables? How is that a protest?

MATT: We refuse to eat and sit in silence, our backs turned to the tables, holding up nutritional labels.

ME: Yeah, have fun with that.

MOM:

DAD (watching the toaster):

MOM (watching his back):

MATT (loudly): I think the protest is really going to make a statement.

ME (nodding): Except that no one will notice. Most of the kids will just keep eating and talking.

MATT: The food is disgusting. And ketchup is not a vegetable!

ME: Hey, so if corn is a vegetable, is popcorn a vegetable?

MATT: No.

ME: Why not?

MATT: It's just not.

ME: That's not a very good answer.

DAD (turning back around): Sweet corn is a vegetable. Popping corn has a different makeup. It's a grain.

ME: Thank you.

MATT: He just said I was right.

ME: Whatever.

MOM:

———

SHRINK: Do things feel different with your mother living apart from you?

ME: Why would you even ask that?

SHRINK:

ME: Yes, it's different. Of course it's different.

———

MATT: Have you heard of unschooling? It's where you leave all of the workbooks and kids sleeping in class and that other crap behind and just educate yourself. You just read books all day and you learn way more than what you get from the one-size-fits-all public school system.

ME: Sounds nice.

DAD: Pancakes or waffles?

MATT: Too many carbs. I'll grab a PowerBar. I think I should drop out of school and teach myself.

DAD: Speaking of which, your school called last night. You can't keep skipping classes.

MATT (eyebrows raised): Last *night*, right . . . whatever. Don't worry about it. I'm counting my absences, making sure I don't get too many to fail.

DAD (staring at him): That's not the point.

MATT: I learn nothing there.

DAD: You're supposed to be getting valuable social skills. Noncognitive something-or-other.

MATT: That's just what they say to make you think this whole thing isn't a giant waste. That our tax dollars wouldn't be better spent on, say, free healthcare and few bucks thrown at the public library and eBooks so kids could read whatever they wanted. I mean, maybe you need school when you're young and learning how to count or read or something, but once you can read on your own, what's the point? They're still teaching that Columbus discovered the world was round. They're actually doing us harm. They—

ME: I want to dropout too.

MATT: You actually *need* those social skills. You have what, *one* friend? If she's home sick, do you even talk to anyone?

ME (glaring):

DAD: Matt, don't be a dick.

MATT: You really shouldn't use that kind of language around impressionable children.

DAD (eyes exaggeratedly wide): Oh, shit, I shouldn't. Fuck!

MATT: Cute. I'm serious about dropping out and you know, educating myself.

DAD: Go to school.

MATT: It's a complete waste of my time.

DAD (rubbing his forehead): I'm tired, Matt. Just go to school.

MATT: If you're tired, maybe you shouldn't stay out all night.

DAD: Matt . . .

He glances pointedly at me.

MATT (waving an arm): It's OK, Dad, she knows.

DAD (meeting my eyes): Fuck. Sorry. (looking straight at me) I'm so sorry.

ME (shrugging): It's fine.

MATT: Let's get out of here. We're going to be late.

———

SHRINK: You and your mother were close.

ME (not blinking): *Are* close.

SHRINK: You must miss her.

ME: Yup.

———

MOM: Sorry, it's a mess.

She's been living here almost two months, and it doesn't look like she's ever cleaned. Her room is strewn with pizza boxes, dirty clothes, an empty bottle or two. She looks just about as bad; her hair is matted and frizzy and standing on end.

ME:

MOM: I wasn't expecting you.

ME (chewing on lip): That's fine.

MOM (hand on her forehead): I'm sorry.

ME: It's fine.

MOM: I've screwed everything up.

I take her hand.

ME: Mom, it's fine. You're fine. You've had a bad year. A really bad year. But everything will be better. I promise. Everything will be better soon.

MOM: I don't deserve you.

ME:

MOM (exhaling): Let me go take a shower, OK?

ME: Sure.

MOM: We can order some pizza, watch a movie.

ME: Sounds good.

———

SHRINK: And your father, do you feel like you can talk to him?

ME: Yes.

———

ME: Mom's lawyer is going to have me testify at the trial.

It's late February, and I'm sitting at a stool behind the kitchen counter, trying to complete a half hour of math homework in five minutes.

DAD (slowly): I don't know if that's such a good idea.

He's standing over by the stove, an open carton of eggs next to him.

ME: I don't know that having my mother ripped away from me and locked up for something she didn't really do and having my father decide to replace her with someone who works at my school is a very good idea either.

He drums his fingers against his chin.

DAD (looking away): OK . . . so, what do you want for breakfast?

ME: Pancakes.

DAD: I'm sorry about . . .

ME (staring at the clock on the stove): It's fine.

DAD: What do you want for lunch?

ME: Money.

———

SHRINK: How do you feel about your parents' separation?

ME: You keep asking these completely obvious questions. What do you want me to say?

SHRINK (smiling one of those fake smiles): There's no right answer. How about you tell me how you honestly feel?

ME:

———

ME: I hate them.

VIVIEN: I know.

ME: I can't believe he would do that.

VIVIEN: You don't know he's cheating.

ME: He's cheating. He more or less admitted it. It doesn't matter. He's screwed everything up.

VIVIEN: It was already screwed up.

It is two in the morning and Vivien has slipped out of her house, ran a mile through the ice-crusted snow, and wound her way up to my attic room. We are lying in my bed, heads propped up on our palms. The only lights are the white Christmas lights my mom and I strung throughout the rafters. Vivien's face dances in the twinkling lights.

ME (blinking rapidly): He could have done more. He could have tried. *She* could have tried. I would give up anything, anything—

VIVIEN: I know.

ME:

VIVIEN:

ME: Matt wants to drop out of school.

VIVIEN: Really?

ME: No, I think he just wants them to think he does.

VIVIEN: So, what, they get back together?

ME: No. I don't know. I don't think he's thought that far.

VIVIEN: It's not a very good plan.

ME: He tells me he's given up on them. That I should just give up. But, I don't know. I don't think he has.

VIVIEN: I think you're right.

ME: It doesn't do any good. Being right.

VIVIEN (leaning her head to the side): It's a moral victory.

ME: He says I should give up my fantasy.

VIVIEN:

ME: In my fantasy, the judge says she's innocent. Bangs his gavel and everything. My dad realizes that he should never have blamed her. It was just an accident, the court said so. They start talking. They remember how good things used to be. They decide to try again. They hold hands. They lay awake at night talking. She comes home.

Vivien touches my shoulder and a shiver runs down my spine.

VIVIEN: I like that.

ME (shaking my head): It's just a fantasy.

VIVIEN: I know.

ME: I don't see how they can just move on.

VIVIEN: I know.

ME: I just can't stop, you know? Thinking it could happen. That they could fix it.

VIVIEN: They could. If they love each other enough, they could.

She reaches a hand out to wipe at my tears.

ME: It will never happen with *her* around.

VIVIEN: So you want to trash her car? My stepbrother has spray paint.

ME (smiling wanly): Sure, right after we rob the corner gas station.

VIVIEN: Hey, for you, I would totally risk my spotless juvenile record. And I bet there's enough cash in that gas station to get us halfway to Chicago.

ME: Which is what, Gary, Indiana?

VIVIEN (shrugging): Pretty much.

ME: No thanks.

VIVIEN: The offer stands, though. I'm up for anything.

ME: Thanks.

Vivien pulls me toward her. She is short and bony and warm. I let myself rest my head on her shoulder.

SHRINK: Do you think your parents will get back together?

ME: I don't know.

SHRINK: And what if they don't? What will that mean?

ME: I don't know. Everything's already changed. Things get worse, or they get better, I guess. Mostly they just get worse.

MOM: Thanks for coming over.

ME: This looks nice.

My mom's room is clean, for once. I think she even got someone to vacuum the carpet. It looks slightly less grungy. The trashcan is empty, save a few gum wrappers and receipts. She is wearing a clean white sweater and jeans. Her blond hair is washed and combed.

She looks like she is supposed to look, like she has always looked.

MOM: Just getting things in order.

ME (forcing a smile): That's good.

MOM: I'm trying.

ME: That's good.

MOM: I'm not drinking.

ME: That's good.

MOM: I'm sorry.

ME: You're fine.

MOM: How's Matt?

ME: He's good. He'll come with me Saturday.

MOM: And your father, how's he doing?

ME (shrugging): Fine. The same.

MOM: How's Vivien?

ME: She's good.

MOM: It's nice you have a good friend.

ME: Yeah.

MOM: It's really nice. To see you happy. With anyone.

ME (shrugging): OK.

MOM: Um, I have to talk to you about something.

I stop breathing.

ME: OK . . .

MOM: It's really not a big deal. Probably better off.

ME:

MOM: Um, I don't want you to testify.

ME:

This isn't what I was expecting. I force myself to suck in oxygen.

ME: Why not?

MOM: I . . . I don't want to put you in that position.

ME (heart racing): It couldn't hurt. I could at least try. That car just came out of nowhere. I saw it!

MOM (hands up, like I am the police coming for her): Maybe.

ME: What do you mean, maybe?

MOM (looking at the ceiling): Your statement to the police . . . you mentioned a house . . . on the corner. There isn't one.

ME: So I was a little confused. I was looking further down the road or something? This is really all about that?

MOM: I made the mistake. Me. It's not your job to fix it.

ME: You can't say that! You can't act like this is all on you when we are all paying for it.

MOM: I know. (running her palm slowly across her forehead as if massaging it) I know. I'm sorry. (looking at me) I will fix this. It might not be the way you want it to be, me and your dad together and all of that, but I will get my life back together. For you, for Matt.

ME: You can't fix it when you're in jail!

137

MOM (not breaking her gaze): I can't fix it by having you lie for me.

ME (standing): I'm not lying!

MOM:

ME: Now? Now you want to fix everything? When it's too late?

MOM: I'm sorry.

ME:

MOM: I will fix this. It's not your job, OK? This is on me.

ME:

———

SHINK: You seem fairly pessimistic about the future.

ME: Yeah, well, my mom might go to jail. My parents hate each other. My brother is pissed at both of them. My dad might get remarried to my school guidance counselor. I don't want some stupid new blended family.

SHINK: That would be the worst-case scenario. And if that did happen—

ME (shaking my head): I don't think there's really any point in talking about this. Accept the things you cannot change. You can't change people.

SHRINK (smirking): Thanks for shooting down my whole profession.

ME (glaring): I thought your job was to help people who want to change. Not to just change people.

SHRINK: True.

ME: I can't change them. I can't keep her out of jail. I can't do anything about anything in my life. There's no point in talking about it.

SHRINK: Talking about it can help you to get OK with the worst-case scenario. There's real value in talking through your feelings.

ME: I think I'm done talking.

ME:

———

VIVIEN: Truth.

ME: What is the most embarrassing thing you have ever done?

Vivien and I are playing Truth or Something. It's our version of Truth or Dare, since neither of us ever takes Dare.

We are lying across her bed in our pajamas, staring at the glow-in-the-dark stars on her ceiling.

VIVIEN: I peed my pants in second grade. And just sat in it because I was too afraid to move. The kid sitting next to me pointed it out. Really loudly. Everyone laughed. And I just kept sitting there, pretending I hadn't. When I finally stood up at the end of the day, everyone could see the back of my pants were soaked. And this was in September. Nine months of them laughing every day. One kid even brought in a diaper for me.

ME: Yikes.

VIVIEN (shrugging): Your turn.

ME: Something.

VIVIEN: Do you believe in God?

ME: I don't know. If he's real, could he just come down and fix my family right now? If he can, then just do it already and I'll believe. If not, then what's the point in having a God?

VIVIEN (shrugging):

ME: Your turn.

VIVIEN: Truth.

ME: Why did you start hanging out with me?

VIVIEN: I watched you. All last year. Does that sound creepy?

ME (smiling): No.

VIVIEN: You looked, I don't know, interesting. That's why I wanted to be your science partner. I wanted to get to know you. But I was scared, so I never really said much to you. I don't know. Then the accident happened.

ME: Yeah.

VIVIEN: Then I figured I had to talk to you. Someone had to. I don't know. I should have a long time ago.

ME:

VIVIEN:

ME: Truth.

VIVIEN: What is your darkest secret?

ME:

VIVIEN:

ME (exhaling): I lied.

ME: To the police.

ME: I dropped my graphic novel on the floor. *Persepolis*. I reached down to get it. Then the car screeched and I banged my head. I didn't see anything.

ME: She hit the gas really fast when we pulled out of the parking lot.

ME: She might have been speeding.

ME: I'm a bad person.

Vivien rests her hand on my wrist. Turns her head to look at me. My stomach quivers.

VIVIEN: No you're not.

ME: The worst thing is, I'm not upset about lying. Even though a girl died. I'm not upset about lying. I'm upset because I screwed up. I told them I was looking at this house on the corner. But I was thinking about the middle school. There's no house on the corner by the high school. I shouldn't have been so specific. If I had just said one thing differently, just one thing . . .

VIVIEN (staring into my eyes): It's not your fault.

ME: I'm a bad person either way.

VIVIEN: You can't put that on yourself.

ME: I couldn't live with myself if I told the truth. I just

wanted to make it all go away. If I hadn't asked her for a ride that day . . .

VIVIEN: It's not your fault.

ME (sighing): No, but I could have prevented it.

VIVIEN: Maybe if you were psychic . . . I think, sometimes, there's a greater truth. Like, you love your mom.

ME: It doesn't matter. She's going to go to jail because of me.

VIVIEN: It won't be because of you.

ME:

VIVIEN: And, even if she does . . . you'll be there when she gets out. It will be OK. You'll be there.

ME: I just wanted to fix everything.

VIVIEN: I know.

ME: I hate that there's nothing I can do.

VIVIEN: I know.

ME:

ME (taking a deep breath): OK, your turn.

VIVIEN: Truth.

ME: What's *your* darkest secret?

VIVIEN:

She turns back away from me to stare at the ceiling. Her hand slips off of my wrist.

VIVIEN (whispering): I think I might be gay.

ME:

VIVIEN:

ME: Good.

She turns back to look at me. She smiles.

Then I silently pick Truth. And reach over. And hold her hand.

And I wonder if we would be having this moment if it weren't for the accident.

The truth is, I'm just as bad as my father.

The truth is, if I could fix it all and make it like it never happened, I wouldn't.

Not if it means giving up Vivien.

I lie there and try to tell myself that I am betraying my mother.

But the truth is, she would just want me to be happy.

So I cry and I laugh, stomach clenched and trembling. And Vivien doesn't say anything, just squeezes my hand and rolls onto her side so she can wipe away my tears with her other hand.

I roll onto my side and study the outline of her face in the dark. The slight curve to her forehead, the small rise and fall of her nose, her lips a snippet of cursive script.

Then I kiss her.

7

THE NEW GIRL

I met them under the worst of circumstances. I had been desperate to get out of school, where no one knew me and I felt completely out of place. I didn't feel like waiting until my mom, who was the newly hired guidance counselor, was ready to leave. I also didn't feel like being seen with her by whomever else was unlucky enough to be stuck at the school past sundown. So when the sports teams started heading home, I went up to the first group of girls I saw and practically begged for a ride.

"I'm Chloe," I remember the nice one with a cheerleader uniform and wild, curly hair saying. She said something about how much she liked the school, or didn't like it, I can't remember which. "Cassie, Kyra, you guys going to say hi at any point?"

They mumbled hellos. Cassie had brown skin, short hair with just a bit of edge to it, and jeans that perfectly hugged her legs. Kyra was built more like me, but every ounce of her was muscle, clearly visible behind a white basketball jersey.

Cassie said something bitchy, like maybe I could walk, but Chloe waved her off. "We can totally give you a ride."

She gave me her seat in the shiny silver car and took up

residence in the back. Which was supposed to be accommo-dating, but it left me with Cassie, who did not want to give me a ride home.

I wanted to jump out, to wait for my mother or at least someone more friendly. But Cassie started the car, and I really wanted to be home, and I figured I could handle the daggers she was psychically flinging at me for the six-minute drive to my apartment.

Then there had been a sharp, sharp noise, a crunching of metal, the *pang* as my teeth banged into one another, the taste of blood.

Screaming.

I spit out blood, then felt my limbs and found they still worked. I undid the seat belt and opened the door, which also still worked. I was able to get out with no discernable pain. I stumbled away from the car and up onto the curb.

Staring at the stark, sand-colored school building, I braced myself for my mother's freak out. I wondered if I could maybe walk away, clean myself up in the bathroom, and pretend not to have been a part of this at all. Some kids got in an accident, everything was fine; I was wandering the halls.

No need for her to freak out. To make me wait, hours, every day after school for a ride.

"Do your homework, Lacey," she'd said. Because she always had the right answer.

Then I looked back.

The perfect silver car looked like something else, crunched up and crushed, like something out of a movie.

And they were still in the car. And there was blood.

They were all moving. Screaming, crying. Bleeding. But they were moving.

People were gathering.

I thought about calling 9-1-1, but I didn't have a cell phone. (My mother thought cell phones were bad for social skills or something.)

I stood there. I stared. I kept thinking I should do something.

All I could do was stare.

At some point, my mother ran up. I heard sirens in the distance.

"Oh my God! Were you in the car?! Oh my God."

I said something about being fine.

They were still in the car.

Then the ambulance came. Or two came, one right after the other. And the police. And a fire truck.

I stared.

The EMTs pulled them out one by one.

Cassie looked OK. Face bloody, hobbling, eyes staring into nothing, but OK.

Kyra had to be carried out, but she looked OK too. She was screaming.

That was probably when the boy ran over. The cops held him back.

Then they pulled Chloe out.

She was bloody. She was not screaming. She was not moving. Her curly hair was bloody. Her leg was bloody. She was not moving.

She had to be OK, though. I mean, this was nothing. The first day of school. They were all talking and laughing and then . . . this was not what happened in the real world. In the real world, the only person I ever knew who died was my seventy-seven-year-old great-uncle who had smoked two packs a day for most of his life. He died two weeks after he quit.

"What a tragedy," my mother had said. "If only he had quit sooner."

Then the boy pulled away and he ran over to where they were strapping Chloe onto one of those yellow plastic boards, the ones they carry people on when they are gravely injured on TV.

He was with her when they got her on the wheeled bed and rolled her past us and into the ambulance.

His head was bent over hers and he was whispering something.

Then they went to lift Chloe into the ambulance.

For a moment, Chloe's eyes locked in on mine. She blinked at me. She saw.

OK, I thought. *She is going to be OK. She will come back to school in a week with crutches and people will cheer. She will be fine.*

"I have to go with you," the boy said. "She's my sister."

"Sorry," the paramedic said. "You have to be eighteen or older."

"Then I'm eighteen," he said.

"Meet us at the hospital," the paramedic said.

That's when the wild girl ran up and held his hand. A blur of colorful hair and patterned clothes.

"That's his sister," she said.

"I don't have a car," he said.

"We can drive you," my mother offered, jumping comfortably into another person's tragedy. "I have to take Lacey to the hospital anyway."

"I'm OK," I said, but she ignored me.

"Thanks," the wild girl said. She looked Asian and was very in-your-face. Black hair streaked with red, done up in high pigtails. Piercings in her eyebrow and nose. Plaid pants and combat boots and a black t-shirt. A polka-dotted backpack.

"Yeah," the boy mumbled. He was dressed simply in jeans and a white t-shirt. Buzz-cut hair. No visible piercings.

"I'm Jade," she said. "This is David."

"I'm parked over here," my mother said, leading us over to faculty parking. I blushed. I had foolishly hoped I could get through all of high school without anyone knowing I was related to the guidance counselor.

David's hands shook.

Once we were in the car, my mother said suddenly, "Oh, we should call your mom!"

"Different mothers," David mumbled.

"Chloe's his half-sister," Jade said. "Same dad, different moms."

"Oh," my mother said. Her mouth hung open for a moment. For a guidance counselor, she really was unprepared for anything out of the ordinary.

"My dad's practically married to Chloe's mom," Jade continued. "I can call him, have him pick her up and bring her to the hospital. She probably shouldn't drive."

"Good," my mother said, looking frantically between them, fingers drumming against her lip. "And what about Chloe's father?"

"He doesn't live around here," David mumbled. "But somebody should probably call him." He slumped down. "And my brother."

"I can call him," Jade said. She had a hand on his shoulder. "OK."

I looked back to see his head between his legs. He was rocking back and forth, ever so slightly.

"She'll be fine," Jade said. She was patting his back. "You know her. She's tougher than she looks. It was a small accident. She'll be fine."

David said nothing.

I latched on to those words. *She'll be fine.* Tomorrow I would wake up and this would all be a dream. A crazy first-day-of-school dream I could tell my dad about when he called on Friday.

Jade made the phone calls.

"Hey Dad, you have to go get Sophie. There was a car accident with Chloe. They're taking her to the hospital . . . I don't know, it didn't look good, but I don't know, they never look good . . . just go get Sophie . . . I know, I know.

"Hey, Travis, this is Jade. I'm like, David's friend or something. Anyway, um, we were at school and there was a car accident . . . no, it was Chloe . . . I don't know; they're taking her to the hospital . . . Bad? We're on our way there, we got a ride. Do you have your dad's number? Oh, OK . . . I guess it's probably better to just go to the hospital . . . OK.

"He doesn't have your dad's number in his cell," Jade said. "It's at home."

David said nothing.

When they finally finished checking me out at the hospital and confirming twice for my mother that I had sustained no damage worse than a broken nail, some bruising, and an already-healing cut on my tongue from where I'd bitten down at the moment of impact, we wandered back into the waiting area and found Jade. She was sitting in one of the worn orange chairs, staring down at her rainbow-colored shoelaces.

"How are you?" my mother asked.

She shrugged without looking at us.

"Where's David?"

"He took off," she said. "Chloe died."

She said it just like that, abrupt.

I stared. I blinked.

My mother tried to hug me and I jerked away.

"Are you OK?" my mother asked Jade.

Jade nodded, a ghost. Stood up shakily and looked toward the door.

My mother hugged her and Jade let her.

This was not supposed to happen.

This was just a bad dream. I would wake up and be back in my old school in Geneva and none of this would have happened.

"I think I'm still in shock," Jade said.

"I know," my mother said. "It's just so tragic."

"I should go find David," Jade said, breaking away from my mother.

"We can stay," my mother said.

I wanted to go home. Curl up under warm blankets and wait to wake up.

"No," Jade said. "David's kind of skittish right now. It will be fine."

"Do you have . . . somebody?"

"Sure." Jade nodded. "My cousin or someone can give me a ride. I'm fine."

"She was your stepsister?"

"Yeah, more or less. But I'm not really close with my dad. So . . ." She shrugged.

"I'm sorry," my mother said. She rested a hand on Jade's shoulder. I kept waiting for Jade to get weirded out by it, to look at me like *What is wrong with your mother?* But she didn't. Because my mother, with her complete lack of cool, is still better at bonding with my classmates than I am.

Jade stared blankly ahead, not registering my mother's hand. "I should go find David," she said again. "Thanks for everything."

"Of course," my mother said.

The Monday after the funeral, Jade and David were back in school. Standing together, almost huddled. I wondered what it must feel like. When they looked up and caught me staring, I looked away.

The other girls I had ridden with—Cassie the driver (broken nose) and Kyra in the back seat (broken leg) weren't back yet. I was dreading the day they returned. They must hate me.

At lunch, I sat alone.

I was the new girl. I had tried imposing myself on people, on forcing friends the way my mother always suggested.

And that had . . . well, there wasn't anything you could say about how that had worked out.

It was a horror.

I was still blinking at the world from behind glassy eyes, like I'd just woken up in the middle of a dream. Still unsure of what had just happened.

From now on, I was just keeping to myself. Head down. Five hundred and thirty-five days until graduation.

Ten days until the new fall TV shows started.

Five days until the weekend.

Two and a half hours until I could go home (but not really, since I'd have to wait another few hours for my mom).

One hundred and eighty-three minutes.

"Hi."

I looked up. There they were.

She was wearing camo pants with a chain belt and a black t-shirt with some sort of CD cover art on it. He was wearing a white t-shirt and jeans.

They didn't have cafeteria trays, just an armful of bags from the vending machine and a pair of sodas.

Nutrition is very important to the growing brain, I heard my mother's voice say.

I pushed it to the back of my mind.

"Hi," I said.

They sat down. Jade popped her soda with a hiss.

I wondered why on earth they were sitting here. With me. Had I taken the last open table? Was I less offensive to sit with than the jocks, pretty people, nerds, and other assorted characters?

I stabbed fruitlessly at my salad with my plastic fork. Rubbed at the gum stuck under the table, then realized what I was rubbing and jerked my hand away.

Jade opened several of the bags.

"Want some?"

I was trying to lose ten pounds. My mother told me I

shouldn't be so hung up on numbers, but that losing a little weight would make me more confident.

I looked at Jade, who dressed in a way that made it clear she loved her curves.

Maybe I was going about things all wrong.

And anyway, those Doritos were calling me.

"Thanks," I said, grabbing a few.

"So this accident is completely fucked up," Jade said. She jabbed at the air with a Dorito.

"Yeah," I said. What else was I going to say?

"You know who the other driver was?" she asked.

"Some lady picking her daughter up from school," I said.

"It was my aunt. Can you believe it? My aunt killed my stepsister. I mean, really. What's worse, she was drunk. Not like, bombed out of her skull or anything, but she's been charged. Manslaughter. Basically murder. Can you believe it?"

"That's crazy," I said.

I noticed David was staring behind me, toward the lone cafeteria window, the bluish gray light from the overcast skies reflecting off his face. I wondered if he could see the accident site from here.

"I know. And then my mom was like, *We stick by family*, and I'm all, *What family?* and then she got all frustrated and left. My mom never asked if my aunt was drunk when she used to drive me and my cousins around. Because, you know, *you stick by family*. Unless the family is me, of course. Then you show them the door."

"What do you mean?" I heard myself ask.

Jade shrugged. "She's always kicking me out. A week, a month, whatever. Her parenting skills are, like, basically giving up and telling me to leave. Or threating to send me away somewhere."

"Wow," I said. "Where do you go?"

The corners of Jade's lips turned upward slightly. "Around. I couch surf, mostly. I used to stay at my dad's or my uncle's, but those are both way too stressful right now. I've crashed at the park before." She shrugged. "So maybe I'll do that the next time she kicks me out."

"You slept in the park?" I asked. "Was it cold?"

She grinned. "It was summer when I did it. I imagine it'll be cold now, though. There's this tunnel-pipe thing I slept in. It keeps the rain off, and no one can really see you in there, like, you know, pedophiles or rapists or whatever."

"Wow," I said again. I was pretty sure my mother still checked to make sure I was in my bed at night. Jade felt about a million years older than me.

"You can always crash at my place," David said.

"Thanks," Jade said. "Maybe when the park gets cold . . . I don't mind staying there," she added. "When I graduate, screw it, I know how to take care of myself."

"So you didn't get hurt or anything?" David asked. All of a sudden he was staring at me.

I blinked a few times. It took a moment to register that he was talking to me, not Jade. "Uh, no," I said. *I was sitting in your sister's seat. If I hadn't been there, she'd be fine too.* "A bruise or two. But nothing."

"Fate is a messed up thing," Jade said.

"I'm sorry," I said.

"You don't need to apologize. Jeez. *I'm sorry I'm alive,* I mean, what is that?" Jade cut in.

David said nothing.

"I mean, I guess I say that to my mom a lot, but it's like, sarcastic. Like, sorry you adopted me; sorry I'm not the nice, compliant, overachieving Chinese kid they advertised; sorry the orphanage screwed me up. Although, personally, I think it was her and my dad. Of course, my sister's like, normal or whatever, so maybe I did come this way. Damaged goods."

"Um . . . OK," I said. I immediately wanted to bang my head against the table. *That* was what I said?

David smirked from behind his soda can.

Jade flashed a wide grin. She leaned forward and hissed, "He's alive."

"Whatever," David said.

Jade kept smiling.

They ate with me every day after that. By Friday, when I saw them already seated, I sat down next to them without a word. I tried not to get too giddy. I had lunch friends.

Kyra had come back on Tuesday, hopping along on crutches. A couple of people tried to help her with things, and she pushed them off, sometimes literally. I heard a rumor that on Wednesday, she'd used her crutch to break a girl's knee. After that, everyone gave her a wide berth.

I always gave her a wide berth. If I noticed her, I immediately looked away.

Cassie had come back on Wednesday. She had two black eyes and tape on her nose. I caught her looking at me once. She might have been glaring. I didn't blame her. If I hadn't taken Chloe's seat . . .

I found myself, sometimes, looking across the room, to where Cassie and her friends sat. Their table was always full. Full with smart kids, full with cool kids, full with popular kids.

Why the hell had I ever thought I could be friends or even friendly with those people?

"You guys want to come over after school?" David asked on Friday.

"Sure," Jade said.

I thought about what my mother would say. Would she need to know the address? Would she insist on driving me there and picking me up? Would she completely humiliate me?

And what would I talk about? I barely had anything to say during a twenty-minute lunch where Jade talked nonstop and I had food shoved in my mouth to provide an easy excuse for not saying anything. What if Jade went to the bathroom?

"You don't have to toke up or anything," David said.

I blinked at him. "Oh, um, OK," I said.

I hadn't even thought about that. What if my mother smelled it on my hair?

David's house was a mile or two from the school, and I managed to convince my mother that walking to a friend's after school was a perfectly normal, safe activity that I could do without her "guidance."

It was still warm out, and Jade entertained us with a few cartwheels along the sidewalk, the chains she wore around her belt clanking as she spun.

The house itself looked old, with peeling paint and a front porch missing half its railings.

Inside, things were messy and cluttered, but not in a *Hoarders* kind of way. I saw a few soda cans on the floor (but not a collection), CDs and videos stacked unevenly against the wall, and, in the next room, a table piled with half-eaten bags of potato chips and empty pizza boxes.

David plopped down on the worn blue couch. "What do you want to watch?" he asked.

"Let's go *Mythbusters*," Jade said. "That cool with you?"

She was looking at me.

"Sure," I said.

"Want anything to drink?" she asked me. "Don't mind David's manners. He has none."

"I'm good."

Jade disappeared into the next room.

"I have manners," David said. "I'm just, you know, mi casa, su casa, or whatever."

"Yeah," I said. "That makes sense."

"You know, you don't have to agree with us all the time," he said.

Before I had a chance to ponder that and determine if it was meant as a criticism or an insult, Jade came back holding three cans of Mountain Dew.

"You're fully stocked," she said. She tossed me a can. "Enjoy the bounty."

I popped the can and sipped, the tiny bubbles tickling the back of my throat.

"So Lacey," Jade said, turning to me and lighting a cigarette. "Why'd you move here?"

I shrugged. "Parents divorced. My mom found a job here. The worst, most humiliating job ever, but . . . yeah, so she dragged me here."

"Oh, your mom's fine," she said with a wave of her arm. "It's cute that she cares."

"She's annoying," David said. "I get the feeling that she wants me to lose it in her office or something. But also that she would have no idea what to do if I did."

"Yeah, but she's new at her job," Jade said, taking a drag off her cigarette. "The last guidance counselor really didn't give a damn. I went in there saying, *I'm homeless, my mom kicked me out*, and he was all, *That's not an excuse to break the vending machine*. I didn't even break the vending machine. I was just hitting it. Dick."

"He was a dick," David agreed. "And he had some weird skin condition."

Jade made a face and turned back to me. "Was your old school this lame?"

"Pretty much."

"You miss your friends there?"

I really did have friends there, once upon a time. Then the stuff with my dad hit the press, and I would come up to find them trying to stop giggling, looking at me with narrowed gazes.

"No," I said. "I kind of hated them."

Jade's eyebrows danced upward, her silver ball-bearing piercing wiggling.

"Intrigue," she said.

"Not really," I said. "They just, I don't know, talked about me behind my back."

"I hate bitches who do that," she said, blowing out smoke. "That's probably why I gravitate toward boys."

"Men," David corrected.

"Boys."

David tossed a pillow in her direction, then turned back to me. "Did your dad stay in Illinois?" he asked.

"Yeah."

"Did you want to stay with him?"

"Not really," I said. "I mean, he drives me a lot less nuts than my mother. But the divorce was definitely his fault, so . . ."

"Who'd he sleep with?" Jade asked. She stubbed her cigarette out in an ashtray.

I froze.

"And you say *I* have no manners," David said.

Jade waved him off. "It's always because someone is screwing around," she said. "Well, not my parents, as far as I know, but most divorces." She turned to David. "Why'd your mom kick your dad out? Because he was sleeping with my stepmom."

David shrugged. "My family is particularly screwed up, though. Chloe and I were less than nine months apart."

I winced at the sound of her name.

But they didn't.

"He slept with a student," I told them. "He was a high school teacher. Not at my school, but in one of the rich neighborhoods. She was eighteen, so it wasn't a crime. Just really, really gross. They couldn't even figure out if they could fire him, so he's still getting paid. Just not going to work."

"Fucked up," Jade said.

"Seriously," David said.

I shrugged. I felt weird. The worst thing that had ever happened to me, at least before the accident, and now it was some sort of street cred. Crappy street cred, but still.

Jade took out a joint after that. Offered it to me; I declined. Offered it to David, who took three hits before reluctantly passing it back.

It smelled a little bit like a freshly cut lawn in the summer.

After they got high, it turned out we didn't have to talk much. They watched TV. I watched them. Jade laughed at everything. David lay his head on the side of the couch and just stared, like he was in a trance or something.

After a while, that became what we did every Friday. Went back to David's, bitched about our parents or the school or the miserable day we were having. Jade smoked a cigarette, then they got high and watched cable.

I did my homework. They didn't seem to mind. David actually cracked me up trying to solve some of the questions while high.

"John F. Kennedy."

"You think JFK was prime minister of the UK during World War II?"

"Absolutely. It's a government conspiracy. They froze him in carbonite. John Wilkes Booth too."

"You know he's the one who shot Lincoln, not Kennedy."

"Or did he?"

Sometimes his mom wandered down, but she didn't seem to care that there were a couple of teenagers getting high in her living room. She always looked like she had just woken up, blinking rapidly, dressed in sweats, hair in tangles.

"She's got like, PTSD or something," Jade said once.

"Or something," was all David said.

In any event, she left us alone.

His brother brought home pizza sometimes, and outside of the occasional question, he left us alone as well.

We spent Saturdays at the park, or the mall or Costco when it got cold. You had to sneak into Costco if you didn't have a membership, act like you belonged to some adult who was going in. Once you were in, they had so many free samples you never got hungry.

I was, occasionally, still stuck eating alone. They'd skip and I'd stay, headphones pressed tightly against my ears, careful to keep my eyes on my plate.

But generally, life was good, so long as I didn't think too long or too hard about why we ever met in the first place.

It was after Jade invited herself over for Thanksgiving that my mother really started asking about them.

"Does Jade have problems at home?" she asked, the door barely closed behind Jade's combat boots.

"Yes, Mom. Doesn't everyone?" The dinner plates clanked as I shoved them into the dishwasher.

"Well, I mean, usually you would spend Thanksgiving with your family . . ."

"Her mom works Thanksgiving," I lied. "And her stepmom wasn't up for cooking."

"I understand," my mother said, in her pseudo-shrink voice. "How is Jade handling things?"

"She's fine, Mom." I rolled my eyes upward, but she wasn't looking.

"And you're also hanging out with David? The brother."

"Yes, Mom."

"Jade's very . . . in-your-face, don't you think?"

"That's what I like about her."

She nodded. She had been running a washcloth down a

glass, but her hands stopped moving. "I understand the desire to make . . . interesting friends. And friends with problems. That maybe you think you can solve."

I gritted my teeth and shoved a bowl into the dishwasher. Backward. "I'm not you. I'm not trying to fix them. They're just my friends. I thought you wanted me to make friends. Or maybe just *your kind* of friends."

"I like Jade and David," she said, "as people. Turn that bowl the other way."

"But they're not good enough for me?" I slammed the dishwasher door shut, leaving the bowl as it was.

She took a deep breath. Went back to scrubbing the glass with the washcloth. "Are they doing drugs?" she asked after a moment.

"The better question, Mom, is am *I* doing drugs? And the answer to that is no. So what does it matter what my friends do?"

She took another breath. "When your friends do drugs, you're more likely to—"

"Mom!" I practically screamed at her. "Either all of your peer pressure lessons worked or they didn't. But you know what? All those nice, preppy kids at school who you want me to be friends with? They're getting high after school. Or popping Ritalin to pass a test. Or taking ecstasy at a club. Or getting drunk, which, according to you, is just as bad. Maybe worse."

She twisted her face around. "If I smell anything on you—beer, pot, anything—"

"Do you trust me at all?" I asked.

"You're a teenager," was her reply.

I took that as an excuse to stomp off to my room and slam the door. It got me out of the rest of the cleanup.

Sometimes, I really hate my mother.

. . .

"Your mom's sleeping with my uncle," Jade said one Wednesday in January after I plunked my tray down at our usual table. Her eyelids were painted in rainbow colors. They waved at me like butterfly wings every time she blinked.

"What?"

"Well, maybe not sleeping with him, but they're definitely dating or getting coffee or whatever. My cousin Matt says that's why his mom moved out. She saw these texts they sent."

"Well, texting is not . . ."

"But she moved out."

I looked to David for help, but he just shrugged and crunched a corn chip.

"She couldn't possibly have moved out over a stupid text," I said. "I mean, she's on trial, isn't she? Maybe it has something to do with that."

"Oh, sure. But it was the texting thing that did them in. He said there's definitely something going on between them. Your mom and my uncle."

I glanced over at Jade's cousin Matt. He was sitting next to Cassie, hand on the small of her back, leaning over to slurp off her straw. I looked away.

"No way," I said. "It sounds like a rumor." I reached for my plastic fork and began jabbing at the congealed ziti on my plate.

"I heard it from Matt," Jade said. "I mean, it's nothing against you. You're not your mother's keeper. I just figured you'd want to know."

"Thanks," I said, gagging on a bite of ziti. What the hell was I supposed to do with that? *Hey Mom, are you by any chance sleeping with the married father of my best friend's cousin?*

My mother, the wronged party in the divorce. My mother, who always knew the right thing to do.

"She, like, practically raised me," Jade said. "My aunt. My mom used to dump me there every day. And then I went there after school all the time. Or when my mom would kick me out. They were all happy. Like joking and laughing and insulting one another. And now it's all . . ."

"I don't really give a shit about your aunt," David said.

"Fuck you."

He shook his head, got up, and left, tossing his half-eaten Fritos in the trash on his way out.

"He'll be back," Jade said. "Don't worry about him."

"OK," I said. I had barely noticed he left.

She drummed her fingers on the table. Her nails were checkered pink and black, scraped and scratched at the tips.

"You probably shouldn't have said that in front of him," I said as my brain slowly caught up.

"Fuck you too," she said. "Look, Lace, you can't baby him. Everyone in his life just side-steps the accident. And what the hell does that get him? His whole brain is full of fucking land mines. Should he and everyone else in the world spend their whole lives tiptoeing around them? Or should we just detonate them all and get it bloody over with? The way I see it, I'm doing a public service."

"Do you miss her at all?" I asked. "Chloe. I mean, you act like you didn't like her, and I know you guys didn't get along . . ."

"When I'm at Sophie's," she said. "I wonder if I'm just vibing it off her, like that's all Sophie sees, so that's all I see, but yeah, I miss her. I miss the way Sophie used to be, and the way her and my dad used to dysfunctionally function. I miss being able to smile around them and not feel like crap. I miss muttering insults at Chloe. I miss hiding her makeup and all those overpriced bottles of gunk just to screw up her morning.

"And you know, sometimes . . . I mean, most of the time, we hated each other, but when my dad got nasty, when he would start calling me a slut and stuff, she, like, she would do things. One time she came out in her little cheerleader uniform and asked how come, if I was such a total slut, I didn't dress more slutty, like her. He didn't know what to say to that. It was kind of funny. She didn't mind calling him a prick or asking her mom why the hell she put up with my dad, right in front of him. She was ballsy like that. Gotta give her respect. I mean, it was easier for her, because he wasn't her dad, but I like to think I'm a badass, and I never told him to fuck off like she did."

She shrugged. "All the stuff David feels about her is complicated. Probably more than mine, and my feelings are all over the place. He loved her, I think, but what does that matter? She's gone. Nothing he can do about it now. He just needs to pack up his shit, label it, and send it off."

I wondered what my mother and her advanced psych degree would say about Jade's philosophy.

Then I remembered that my mother might be sleeping with a married man, and I decided that I really didn't care what she would say.

I didn't say anything to my mom. What was I supposed to say? *Hey Mom, are you having an affair?* Does it count as an affair if she's not the one who's married?

I looked around a bit. Checked the laundry for men's socks. Tried unsuccessfully to guess her iPhone security code (apparently not my birthday). Looked through her underwear drawer, because that was where Jade said people of her generation hid things.

I got nothing.

I figured Jade's cousin was lying or mistaken or thinking of someone else. I didn't say it to Jade, of course. But he had to be wrong.

Then, two months after she first told me the rumor, I woke up at two in the morning to use the bathroom and heard noises coming from my mother's room. *Those* kind of noises.

I skipped the bathroom and crept across the beige carpeting, returning to my bed, where I lay staring up at the water stain the ceiling, waiting. Waiting to hear him leave.

Eventually I got up and surfed the internet.

The room turned a pale, dusky gray.

Then I heard the bedroom doorknob turn. The footsteps. Silence. Then the sound of the toilet flushing. Another door. A few minutes later, the front door. I went to my window and looked out at the parking lot. I couldn't make out his face when he emerged, but I saw the car. A green Ford Taurus. With a yellow bumper sticker.

I was a zombie through breakfast.

I decided I wouldn't speak to her, but she didn't seem to notice. She was humming in the corner of the kitchen, then reading the paper while she ate her shredded wheat.

I hated her. For real this time.

I was supposed to have the normal, pain-in-the-ass mother. She paraded around, telling everyone what to do. Her fancy degree. How the hell was she talking to us every day, to *me* every day, telling us what to do, what we were doing wrong? Who the hell was she to judge Jade or me or my dad or anyone?

I found Jade before we got to first period. "Let's ditch," I said.

She stared at me. "Seriously?"

"Does your uncle drive a green Taurus with a yellow bumper sticker?" I asked.

"Fuck," she said. She laughed a little.

"Let's ditch," I repeated.

"Let me find David," she said. "Meet me out back."

"Um, how do you, you know, get out of here?"

She giggled. "OK, come with me." She hooked her elbow around mine and pulled me down the hall, our sneakers squeaking. A few minutes after the bell, we found David in bio lab. On Jade's orders, I eased open the door and said, "Um, hi, we need a, um, David Miller to come to the office."

David was sitting behind a black table and flicking a Bunsen burner on and off. He looked at me with a raised eyebrow.

The teacher waved him out without looking up.

"What's going on?" he asked in the hall.

"She finally believes me," Jade said. "About her mom."

"I kind of heard them," I said.

"Yikes," he said, laughing and grimacing all at once.

Jade pulled me down a series of hallways until we found ourselves in the theater. It was empty, and beautiful in its decadence. Red, velvet-covered seats.

"Remind me again why we have assemblies in the gym," I asked.

Jade shrugged. "I think this is just for show. Can't have the kids running wild in here, leaving their chewed gum and dirty shoe prints everywhere."

She led us down the aisle, up to the shining wooden stage, and behind the red velvet curtain, then out a door labelled *exit* in glowing red letters and into the sunlight, harsh against the stark white snow.

"They don't lock the door?"

She shrugged. "Depends on the day. There are three good ways out of this place: the theater, the old art room if there isn't a class, and the back of the cafeteria after the crew leaves. If those fail, then you just have to run past a hall monitor. Which isn't hard; they're mostly retired people. And they're afraid to touch a student, because we'll like, totally sue."

"Doesn't the hall monitor report you?"

She looked at me. "So?"

And then I shrugged and said, "Yeah, I guess I don't really care."

We went to David's house. This time of year we walked quickly; it was too cold to cartwheel and joke around.

"How did you find out?" Jade asked. She was slouched into the sofa, eating a Twinkie.

"He was over basically all night."

"And you woke up and like, heard them doing it?" David asked.

"Shut up, I'm trying to block it out."

He snorted. Jade laughed.

"Shut up," I said. I was laughing too. "This is very traumatic."

"I'm sure it is," Jade said. "I mean, your parents are not supposed to have sex. Once you're born, that's it. Never again."

"Shut up."

"I'm sure this is very hard for Lacey," David said. "Up until now her life has been all *Leave It to Beaver* and shit."

"You know it hasn't."

"Compared to our lives, your life is pretty goddamn normal."

"Well, I don't care about comparing my life to your lives. This is a big deal to me. My mom does not go around breaking up marriages. I mean, she should know how that feels. I don't know what the hell is wrong with her."

"My aunt and uncle are separated now," Jade said. "So I don't know. Sometimes you're allowed to have sex with other people when you're separated."

"She always acts like she's so much better than everyone," I said. "So much better than me. It's just complete bullshit."

Jade grinned. "You're just now figuring this out?"

"Shut up."

Jade giggled. "I still like your mom," she said. "She's just human or whatever." She wedged the last of the Twinkie into her mouth.

"I want to get high," I said.

"Seriously?" David propped himself up on an elbow and looked at me.

"No way," said Jade. "You want to piss off your mom. And you're ditching school at a school where she works. So, mission accomplished. You still want to get high next week, I'll buy you your first joint. I am *dying* to see you high. But I'm not going to be one of those pushy bitches from those after-school specials."

"Who's being pushy? I asked for it."

"I'm not taking advantage of your emotional state."

"Fuck you."

"Don't mind if you do." Jade grinned. A piece of spongy yellow cake was stuck to her teeth. "I'm an equal-opportunity slut."

I looked at David and he shrugged.

I snorted. "Fine," I said. "Let's just watch something."

We settled into a moody silence. I was tired, having been up half the night, and found myself drifting in and out of sleep, the different offerings of daytime TV stitching themselves together into a meandering, dream-like narrative. The Mythbusters ran experiments to determine that "Rick, you are the father." Judge Judy ruled that Jerry Seinfeld owed Elaine $1100 in back rent.

Jade got a text and tapped something into her phone. "Sophie wanted to know if I'd be home for dinner," she said. "I'm assuming not, since you need me."

"Whatever," I muttered.

"You living there now?" David asked.

"Mostly." She shrugged. "My mom and I are getting along a lot better when we only see each other in small doses. And Sophie's great. You should come by sometime."

"Just drop it."

"She'd like to see you. You don't have to have some whole *thing*. Just go there and say hi and whatever. You're sort of family."

"No, we're not." David pushed himself forward on the couch and fixed his eyes on Jade. "My mom never wanted us around her. The reason my dad stopped taking us all to the beach every summer was because I told Chloe her mom was a slut and then she didn't really want to hang out with me anymore. I told her it a whole bunch more times, too, in school and wherever. I was a little asshole. I really don't think her mom wants to see me."

"First of all, I doubt Chloe told her—" Jade started.

"So, what, I'm supposed to go over there and pretend? Oh yeah, Chloe and I got along so well . . . just like a real brother and sister. I never wrote mean things about her on the bathroom walls. I never stole her candy at school. I was a good brother, I looked out for her. I beat up the guys who talked crap about her and I made her cards and cookies for her birthdays. Who the hell is that supposed to make feel better?"

"You can just talk about the good times. I know there were good times. And I was just as horrible to Chloe. Probably worse. You can still love someone and be a total bitch to them."

"She was my sister." He hit a button on the remote and, with a snap of static, the TV was suddenly dark. "Not my almost-stepsister or whatever. My *sister*. My blood. We were supposed to care about each other. We were supposed to play Monopoly and fight over the cereal prize and get each other Christmas gifts and shit. We didn't do any of that. You want to know what the last thing I said to her was? It was last spring and I was high for the assembly and she called me a stoner loser and I called her a bitch. And then we just didn't talk and not because we were pissed, but because we didn't care that much. And then she died. Like nothing. She just died."

Jade said nothing.

"If you don't mind, I'd really rather not go see her mother, who actually acted like she loved her. I'd rather not hear all of the actually nice things she has to say about her. I'd rather not be reminded of what a dick I am."

Jade was silent. She picked at the black polish on her fingernails.

"You loved her," I said, sitting upright on the worn blue couch. "Jade's right—you can be a bitch to someone and still love them."

"And what does that get me?" His eyes were glassy. "She's dead. The last thing I ever said to her was *bitch*. There's not a nice spin you can put on that."

"It's my fault she's dead," I said. I didn't mean to.

They looked at me.

I knotted my fingers together into the same tight formation as my guts. "I took her seat. She gave me her seat. I didn't want to wait for my mom so I asked them for a ride. She was supposed to be sitting where I was. Even if the timing was the same, she'd be alive. She'd be fine. A couple of bruises, nothing."

They stared.

"Yeah, and if a butterfly flapped its wings in Indonesia, she'd still be alive," Jade said, throwing her arms out wide. "You can't blame yourself for that. If my cousin Jenna hadn't wanted a ride home, if my aunt hadn't decided to have one more drink, if stupid Cassie had bought a safer car . . ."

"Shut up," I said to Jade. I kept looking at David.

"What the hell am I supposed to do with that?" he said. He pulled at his lower lip with his thumb. "I know it was your fault. And Cassie's fault, and Jade's aunt's fault, and her cousin's, and everyone in the fucking world. I'm sure if you trace it back far enough, it was my fault. What do you want me to say? *Screw you, if it weren't for you, my sister that I barely spoke to would still be alive?*"

I shrugged. I did not want him to say that.

"Well, I'm still glad I met you, and I wish to God you

hadn't asked for a ride." He exhaled, then made a sort of half-laughing, half-insane sort of chuckle.

"It's messy," Jade said.

"No shit."

"I'm sorry," I said.

"I know," he said. He met my eyes. "I forgive you."

"Thanks."

"You shouldn't have to apologize for something like that," Jade said. "It's not like you knew—"

"Still," I said. "It happened."

"It's not like I made her apologize," David said. "I mean, I agree, I guess, but you know, if you feel bad about something, you should friggin' say it. Not wait until after the person's dead. Not much you can do with that."

"You talked to her, though," I said. "Chloe. After the accident. So that wasn't the last thing you said to her."

"She couldn't hear me," he said. He looked down. There was a broken piece of Dorito on the floor.

"Yeah she could. She looked right up at me when they put her in the ambulance. She could hear you."

He swiped his hands beneath his eyes and nodded. When he looked up at me, I saw the sunlight dance and sparkle in his eyes.

"Thanks."

After a few moments of what Jade called awkward silence, David turned the TV back on. I fell back asleep. Bob Saget told his kids how he met their mother with the help of Scooby and Shaggy and the gang.

I awoke to Jade gently shaking my shoulder. "Your mom called my cell," she said.

"Seriously?"

"I told her you were fine and we'd have you home by dinner."

I closed my eyes. "Shit."

"The whole point of today was to piss her off, right?"

"I don't know, I guess. I just don't want to deal with her."

"Unless you want to be even more homeless than me, I think you have to," Jade said. "It's like a rite of passage. You scream at each other, doors get slammed. In my house occasionally a knife gets thrown . . ."

"What?!"

"Not at the person, just, I don't know, near them. To be dramatic and all. Not like trying to stab them or cut them or anything."

"That's messed up."

"Told you your stuff was nothing."

They walked me home through the crunching snow, which was nice. Left me in front of the building. Jade gave me a quick hug and David patted my shoulder.

My mother was pacing back and forth across the tiny living room when I got in. She whirled around to face me.

"What. Was. That?" she asked. "Why. Were you. Not in school?"

"I was tired," I said, sliding off my coat. Then, "You and your visitor kept me up all night."

She stared. Her eyes bugged out.

"I just slept for a few hours at David's," I said. "Hand to the Bible." I hung my coat by the door.

"You," she said, "you can't just do that. You can't just leave school without my permission, without even telling me. Do you know how worried I was? What went through my mind?"

"If you let me get a cell phone, I could have texted," I said.

"Cute," she said. "You are never getting a cell phone. Never."

"What, are you afraid I'm going to start texting married men?"

Her mouth resembled that of a trout that's just been reeled out of the water.

"Lacey! Oh, you need to sit down and just listen. I think

you've heard some rumors and—" She started to sink into the chocolate brown sofa.

"Don't," I said. "Don't act like that. Like you're so much better than me. Like I'm just some confused, dumb little kid. He's married, you guys were flirting, but hey, maybe you weren't sleeping together, so no harm? Now his wife moves out and you move in. You know he's not even divorced? And he has two kids. Who go to my school. He's Jade's uncle."

"That is why we've been trying to keep it quiet, so we wouldn't upset you," she said in that same cloying voice. "His marriage is over, trust me. And it had nothing to do with me. They'd had trouble communicating for years. And then she was drunk and—"

"I know, Mom. I was there."

"We're not doing anything wrong."

"Of course not. It's all perfectly legal, all perfectly ethical. No one's getting hurt."

"I can't help how his kids feel." She flung her arms into the air. "Or how you feel. But we are trying very hard not to hurt anyone."

"Great work."

"You know what I think? I think this is a distraction. You've clearly known about this for some time. You want to skip school and you think it's OK because you have this. It is not. It is completely unacceptable. It—"

There was a pounding on the door.

She glared, then went to answer it.

It was Jade.

"Ms. Simms, hi," Jade said. "I'm really sorry, but I really need Lacey. I know you guys are having a, like, really important fight right now or something, but it's an emergency. Our friend David is, like, having this total crisis. You know how weird and messed up his family is, right?" Jade spread her arms wide. "And now his dad is saying that maybe he's not even his dad or something. Like, he wants DNA. And David is freaking out, of course. And, like, I don't know what to say. But Lacey is so good at this stuff . . . I think she picks it up from you or something. And they've gotten really close; she's really helped him out with all the Chloe dying stuff . . ."

My mother blinked at her.

Jade gave her an encouraging smile.

"This just happened?" she asked.

"Yeah, like, his dad came over right after Lacey left. I swear, he's about to lose it."

My mother massaged her forehead. "Does his mom know where he is?"

"Oh yeah, I texted her. So she wouldn't worry."

My mother attempted a smile. "That was thoughtful of you."

Jade smiled. "I know you're pissed at Lacey, and you totally have every right to be. She should have at least texted you. But we, like, really need her right now. Please?"

My mother ran her hands through her hair. She looked at me. Her gaze wandered up and down.

"Um . . . I guess . . . maybe for a little bit? Can you call me in an hour and let me know what's going on?"

"Oh, definitely. Thank you so much. You are the best. I mean, seriously, I was just telling Lacey how nice it was that she has a mother who cares as much as you do. Not just about her, but about, like, all of us." She smiled again.

"Thanks," my mother said, her head bobbing like she was waiting for the catch.

"Um, thanks, Mom. Bye," I said hurriedly, grabbing my coat and darting out the door.

Jade grabbed my hand and dragged me down the hall, where David stood, grinning and waving.

"What the hell was that?" I whispered, pausing to put on my coat.

"I figured you could use a break," she said, turning toward

me. "You'll both calm down and when you get back you'll both be done screaming and you'll just be grounded and you can get on with ignoring each other. And then you'll get over it."

"Super," I said, shaking my head.

"Are you not grateful?"

I looked at them. Jade was wearing an old army jacket, too thin for a night like tonight. Lollipop sticks poked out of the pockets. David was in a thick Carhart jacket that looked two sizes too big for him. His fingers twitched, as if searching for a joint.

I grinned. "Let's get out of here," I said.

Jade whooped. I hoped my mother didn't hear.

"You know she's dragging you into her office tomorrow," I said to David as we crossed the parking lot. "To check in with you and make sure everything's OK."

"Cool. I'll ask her if she thinks we should go on *Maury* for the free DNA test."

"You say that, she'll probably call your parents in."

"How long does it take DNA tests to come back?"

"Weeks, I think."

"Then I think I need counselling until then. It's giving me a lot of anxiety. Can you have her get me out of gym? I hate gym."

"Forget the DNA thing," Jade said. "She knows your family's messed up. You'll get over that. What you need to do is tell her that you're in love with Ms. Warner. And that going to gym class and seeing her every day is causing you great psychological distress."

"Ms. Wart-nose?"

"She really does seem like your type, now that I think about it."

"Now I'm picturing the two of you , , , ugh!"

"I really think it speaks to your level of taste, in that you have none."

"That would explain why I'm friends with the two of you," David muttered.

"Oh, fuck you."

We crossed the street and made a beeline for the parking lot, the crisp night air stinging the backs of our throats.

And, just for a little bit, we were free.

8

THE LONGEST WINTER

October

Sophie would wake in the morning with a feeling of panic at the back of her throat. She would swallow it down and focus on her breathing. In and out, in and out. The sky was always gray when she woke up, the clouds pregnant with the possibility of rain.

It was always too cold. She would turn the thermostat up, and then Bob, her boyfriend, would turn it down. "It's only October," he would point out, like the date was supposed to mean something. Like the weather was supposed to keep a regular schedule. "We can't afford to heat the apartment in *October*." He paid everything now. The last time Kelly had called, she had said the job was still there, any time she wanted it. But that had been over a month ago. Sophie wasn't going back.

She pulled the blankets over her head, cupped her hands around her mouth. Felt her warm breath tickle her fingers. And shivered anyway.

Her back ached, her feet ached, and her hip ached.

She should get up.

But then again, there was no reason to get up.

No job to shower for. No one to cook breakfast for. No child to get off to school.

She shivered under the blanket and prayed for sleep to return.

As always, her prayers went unanswered.

The pills they had given her—some rejected anti-depressant that worked wonders as a non-addictive sleeping aid—only worked for so long.

The problem with being awake was that her head stubbornly refused to lie still. Her body was more than acquiescent, but her mind wandered. It never really wandered far. Just followed the well-worn route—past the danger signs, the cobbled together chicken-wire fence—over to Chloe.

The shape of her face. Cheeks still smooth with not-quite-shed baby fat, colored pink with blush. The lips, curled up into a smile. Her too-small nose. The holes she had insisted on putting in her earlobes, usually adorned in knock-off sapphire. Her eyes, dark and deep.

And then she had to push it away. Swallow hard. Blink repeatedly. Breathe out through clenched teeth.

She gathered the blanket around her and padded down the hall to the living room. Made sure the remote was where she'd left it, on the side table, and lowered herself, shivering, onto the brown-and-tan sofa.

Tried not to remember the way she had pushed the couch back against the wall so Chloe could have enough floor space to show off her cartwheels or handsprings or whatever new trick she had picked up. Giggling—corkscrew curls gathered into a ponytail—and springing off the ground as she flipped.

She reached for the remote and flicked on the TV.

MSNBC. Bob must have been watching. She felt the familiar tightness in her lungs. She wondered if Chloe had made the evening news last month. She wondered what the papers had said. She wondered if she should have had someone pick one up. Saved a copy. The capstone to the scrapbook she had started just before the accident. The one that was meant to cover Chloe's high school years, ending with graduation. To be displayed on the coffee table at the open house celebrating the end of her childhood, her academic success, her bright horizons.

She clicked the channel up.

HGTV. Still dangerous. The programs tended to make her think about how she should move. Get away from the spaces that trapped her in her grief. And how she couldn't move. She didn't have a job. She didn't have a security deposit. She didn't have the mental energy to look for an apartment. And she didn't even want to think about Chloe's room. And putting it all into boxes.

And really, she was a bad mother for wanting to move. For praying to forget about her daughter, even a little bit. For wanting to come home one day and find everything changed and new, all of her things in boxes stowed away in the attic they didn't have. The living room in a different place with a different couch. Every last memory wiped clean.

If she was going to be forced to start a new life, she wanted it to look new. She wanted to know, immediately, that everything was different now, not be reminded over and over again in tiny moments.

She wanted to yank the Band-Aid off.

And yet.

The gaping black gulf beneath terrified her.

What was she, without Chloe?

She'd gotten pregnant when she was nineteen. Eddie was already married, to a woman he kept promising to leave. He just stayed for his son. But then she had gotten pregnant, so she figured he would do the math and leave. He might have, too. He said he was going to. Then his wife got pregnant again.

Her parents made their disapproval clear. Her sister and

brother were too young to do anything but follow their parents' lead.

So it had been her and Chloe, more or less alone. Eddie showed up for the birth, wide grin spreading across his stubbly face. He sent money from time to time. He'd stop by and take Chloe out for ice cream or on a camping trip.

But still. That first night, in the hospital, she had been all alone. Staring at the tiny person in the plastic bassinet beside her. Watching the spot on her neck that moved in and out with each breath. Wondering why here, in a hospital, there was nothing hooked up to this tiny person to alert them if she should stop breathing. Being so exhausted she could barely think, but unable to close her eyes, jerking awake every few moments. Searching for that spot on her neck.

And she had been alone at five in the morning when Chloe had woken up bawling, alone in trying to drag her sore and too-tired body out of bed, alone in lifting the tiny creature from the plastic encasing, alone in stumbling to the rocker to nurse. She had been alone hours later, trying to keep from dozing off sitting up, babe attached to her breast, singing made-up songs, praying she would just go back to sleep.

She had been alone when Chloe had finally drifted off and stopped suckling, alone in stumbling to her feet, alone in slipping the small child back into the bassinet. Alone in that small victory.

She'd taken hold of that. She would do it all. She would be stronger for doing it alone. She would need no one.

When Eddie's wife found out and kicked him to the curb and he came crawling back to Sophie, she'd said no. Shut the door in his face. She didn't need him anymore.

Chloe was her stunning accomplishment. One that belonged to her and her alone. Years later, checking the progress of her nieces and nephews on Facebook, she would feel a surge of pride. She may not be married or own a house, but for all of her mistakes, her daughter was better than they were. She crawled sooner than her cousin Milo. She laughed more than Elaina. She knew twice as many words at that age than Maddox.

She had done a good job with her daughter. Polite, good grades, lots of friends. She could be difficult at home, high-strung and temperamental, but weren't all teenage girls? Her teachers, her coaches, everyone said she was a delight to work with. Bob even liked her, and he seemed completely done with teenage girls after the hell his own daughter had put him through, smoking, drinking, dropping onto their couch in the dead of night, only to slip away while he was at work, not to resurface for weeks.

"You're so lucky to have her," Bob would say of Chloe. "You're so lucky to know she's safe and that she loves you."

And now it was all gone.

As strong and independent as she liked to think she was, she had been completely dependent on Chloe. Completely dependent on God, on the world, to keep her baby safe. Exposed, naked, vulnerable.

Everything she loved, the very thing that defined her, sent out the door every morning, into the world, with no more than a thin layer of skin and bone to protect her.

Gone now. Her every accomplishment wiped away, like it was never even there.

And then of course, the guilt. Who was she to think about Chloe in this way? As a part of her? As Sophie's world, Sophie's future? Hadn't Chloe had her own dreams? Hadn't she wanted to go to college in California? To be a doctor or an actress or a high-end fashion designer? Hadn't she wanted one of those bright stucco houses on the beach they showed on these programs, with big windows that faced an ever-present sun? Hadn't she wanted to fall in love, get married, feel her own baby pressed against her breast?

Once upon a time, there had been a person here, a

giggling, shrieking, unpredictable person. And now there were memories. And dreams that would never be. And her own life, with no one to share it with and nothing to show for it.

Bereft.

She changed the channel again. The Food Network. Better.

December

Sophie woke up cold, sheets and blankets wrapped tightly about her shivering form. She stared at the clouds her breath formed.

It was snowing outside, but Bob still insisted they set the thermostat no higher than sixty-five degrees. They had been together five years, and this was the first winter she remembered it being an issue.

"I'm cold," she had said. That should have settled it.

"Get a blanket," he'd said, arms folded across his chest.

She had looked at him with rounded eyes.

"I'm sorry," he had said, leaning over to stroke her face. "I just can't . . . they keep cutting my hours . . ."

"A blanket will be fine," she had told him.

She lay under a pile of blankets now, shivering.

Her hair was unwashed, in greasy tangles about her head. She should shower, she thought.

The warm water would be nice.

But that would mean getting up. Venturing into the cold.

Bob poked his head in. He was showered and dressed, wearing a red polo shirt. "Do you want coffee?" he asked.

She shook her head, but he didn't seem to see.

"Sophie? Do you want coffee?" The light he'd turned on cast a glare off his balding head.

"No," she whispered. She covered her face with her hands for warmth.

"You can't keep doing this," he said. "You need to get up. You need to shower."

"Later," she said. "I have a headache."

"Coffee will help."

"I don't want coffee."

"Did you eat anything last night?"

She shook her head. This time he noticed.

"You can't keep doing this to yourself!" he shouted.

She trembled.

"You need to get your stuff together," he said more quietly. "I can't keep watching this. You don't let me help you, and I'm not just going to watch . . ."

She stared at the blur her fingers made, so close up to her face.

He didn't say anything more, just stomped around the kitchen, making coffee in the loudest way imaginable. Then out the door, pulling it closed with the force of a small truck.

The reverberations of the slammed door, a minor earthquake, still echoed in her ears.

She curled into a ball and cried. *My daughter just died, my daughter just died,* she repeated to herself.

You're an ass, she thought to Bob.

She finally made it out to the brown-and-tan couch, blankets wrapped around her shoulders.

She should eat something.

But that meant getting up. Moving.

Then Bob's daughter Jade stopped by. Wild, beautiful, out-of-control Jade.

"You should be in school," she said, secretly delighted that Jade was not.

"Gas leak," Jade said unconvincingly, dropping her polka-dotted backpack near the door. "Mind if I take a shower?"

"Of course not," she said, wheels churning. "Where have you been sleeping?"

"You know, here and there." Jade shrugged, running a hand through her red-streaked black hair.

Nowhere with a shower.

Still, Jade looked cleaner than Sophie imagined she herself looked.

"You should stay here," she said. Jade stayed there a lot these days.

Jade shrugged. "I don't need him up my ass." She was talking about Bob. This meant she would probably leave, then come back after Bob had gone to bed. Or maybe not. Some nights she didn't come back.

Sophie tried not to worry.

Tried not to get attached.

"He just cares about you," Sophie said.

"He's an ass."

Sophie smiled in spite of herself. While Jade was in the shower, she made tea and microwaved some popcorn. They sat and watched a *Chopped* marathon.

"This is making me hungry," Sophie admitted.

"You need to eat more," Jade said. "You look thin."

"It is a great diet," she heard herself say. "Grief."

Jade looked at her, a tooth biting against her lower lip. Then she grinned.

They sat in silence for a few minutes.

"You have to be a tough bitch to win this show," Jade said finally, her freshly washed hair making a wet spot on the back of the sofa.

"Every woman has to be hard," Sophie agreed. "If you are delicate . . ." She shook her head and Jade nodded.

She remembered how delicate her emotions had been during Chloe's first weeks of life. A thin membrane, like a fine web of spun sugar, the only thing holding back her emotions. Anything could make her cry. The sight of the free copy of

Parenting magazine that they had somehow known to send her. The warmth of her sleeping daughter in her arms, the steadiness of her breathing. The flyer raising money for a boy in town who had been struck by a car while practicing for cross country and was now in a coma.

Jade made mac and cheese for lunch.

"Here," she said, handing Sophie a steaming bowl. "It's not exactly fine cuisine."

"It's delicious."

"You must be desperate," Jade said. She twisted her eyebrow piercing between her thumb and forefinger.

"Hunger is the best spice; that was what my mother used to say."

She reminded herself, again, of what Bob had said that morning. How she needed to start taking care of herself. She wondered if, or when, he would leave her.

She felt a tightening sensation in her gut. She was already so alone. She couldn't imagine sliding into bed at night, the nights she made it to bed, without the warmth of another human being.

Or Christmas. Her first without Chloe. How would she ever get through that day alone?

She wondered who would notice if she never got out of bed.

And she wondered what would happen if she never spoke to another human being again. She wondered if she would really even exist at that point.

"Does he ever cook?" Jade asked.

"He microwaves," Sophie said with a shrug.

Jade laughed. It was a beautiful sound, light and musical.

"I should take a shower," she said after a bit.

Then she found herself getting off the couch. Padding down the hallway. Stripping off her sweat pants and thermal shirt and stepping slowly into the almost scalding water.

At first, the hot water seemed to bounce off her skin. She could feel it was hot, but her skin felt too cold to receive its warmth, like hot and cold were magnets, repelling each other. Gradually, though, she felt herself relax.

She thought about the flowers Bob brought to their first date. That nervous smile on his face, the way his hand had shaken ever so slightly when she brushed up against it. She thought about the way, months later, Bob had broken down and cried talking about the way Jade was living, the way he felt powerless to do anything about it. She thought about how all these months he had paid the bills, made the food, done everything, really, without much complaint, while she had curled up under the blankets and shut the world out. Shut him out.

He was a good man, she reminded herself.

And then she let herself think just a little bit further. And picture something else. Something more.

By the time the hot water ran out, only her feet were still cold.

She wiped the mirror clean, then attacked her hair with the comb and gel. Applied eyeliner, deodorant.

There were no clean clothes.

"I'm going to run down to the laundry room," she told Jade.

"Let me do it; you're wearing a towel."

She looked down, scrunched her face together, smiled. "Thank you."

While she waited for Jade, she started dinner. There was chicken in the freezer, plus vegetables. She could make something with that.

By the time Jade came back with the laundry, there was a pleasant smell in the kitchen. Garlic and parsley wafted through the apartment.

"Wow," Jade said, her studded eyebrow arching.

"You want to stay for dinner?"

Jade shook her head. "I should go," she said. "Give you two a nice night alone."

"Where will you go?"

"I have friends," Jade said with a shrug. "Don't worry about me."

She started to say something else, but didn't. Bob had always said there was no use in trying to pin Jade down, trying to keep her safe. She broke your heart every single time.

After Jade left, she set about folding the laundry. She found a pair of Chloe's jeans, a bra. She pushed past them. She would put everything away. Change the sheets. Clean the floors. Serve a delicious dinner. Bob would come home and be impressed. They could start fresh. A new beginning.

The future would open up.

Bob came home late, but seemed happy with dinner.

"This is good," he said, looking at her. "You look really beautiful."

She radiated.

He talked about work, how the boss just didn't understand how the job was done, how hard it was to keep all of the damn store managers happy.

She nodded.

She had nothing much to say. She didn't work. She didn't watch the news. She couldn't tell him Jade had stopped by; it would just upset him. He worried, in spite of himself.

After dinner they caught the second half of the first *Lord of the Rings* movie on cable. She snuggled into his arms and tried to not pay any attention to the plot line.

When they slid into bed, he kissed her deeply. She felt his tongue inside her mouth. Warm, pulsing, alive.

"Do you want to?" he asked, eyebrows raised.

She nodded.

He used a condom. Which saved her the trouble of admitting she hadn't bothered to refill her birth control.

Afterward, they lay there, her head on his chest.

"I love you," he breathed.

"I love you too," she whispered.

She felt warm, truly warm, for the first time in ages. Even her toes.

"Do you think," she whispered, "not now, of course, but in a little bit, in a while, maybe, maybe we could have a baby?"

From beneath her cheek, she felt his chest tense. His heart beat more rapidly.

She left her head where it was. Held her breath.

"It's not a dog," he said. "You can't just get a new one."

Tears sprung into her eyes. She jerked her head off his chest. Sat naked in the darkness.

She waited for him to say something, to apologize.

She waited.

"Look," he finally said, reaching out to stroke her face. "I loved Chloe too. But we can't bring her back. You can't just replace her. We just need to focus on the future. You and me. You go back to work; we'll get some more money coming in. We can go up to Traverse City, or maybe over to Chicago. Have a nice vacation. Start enjoying ourselves."

She pulled away from him, her heart sinking downward toward the cold stones that were now her toes. "You have no idea," she said. "If you loved her, you would not be able to talk about the future. To think about having fun like that. Without her." She shook her head. "Get out," she said, trying not to let her voice betray the tears that streamed down her face.

"What?"

"Get your things and leave."

"I loved her," he said. "I know it's harder for you, but what you're doing to yourself, it's not helping. I'm sorry I'm the more practical one, but you need to move on with your life."

"That was what I was trying to do," she whispered.

"Look at my kid!" he exploded, jabbing at the air. "Look how she turned out. I'm no damn good with kids."

"That is true," she said, wrapping the blankets tighter. "I should never have picked you. I should have waited for someone who was good with kids. That was my mistake."

His face turned red. She could see it in the darkness.

"What the hell? Are you that twisted? You just want another baby to replace her? And, what, I won't give you one, so screw this? You'll find someone who will?"

"You are an asshole," she said, trying to sound sure of herself. She wrapped the comforter around her shoulders.

"Good luck trying to find someone to put up with your shit. Pay all the bills, clean the bathroom, watch you lay around all day, greasy hair and filthy fingernails. Real sexy. Yeah, I'm sure they'll be lining up to put a baby in you."

She trembled and sobbed and waited for him to leave.

January

Sophie rose to find she still occupied the right half of the bed, even though Bob was no longer there to take up the left.

It had been a month, and she found herself surprised to miss him.

But still determined not to call him.

She breathed in deeply, enjoying the crisp, clean steel of the air.

She had always been weak in the winter, too cold, too tired, too often on the edge of a bad head cold.

Now, though, in the midst of a polar vortex, she felt warmer.

She had cranked the heat to seventy-five.

She hit the alarm to make it stop bleating. She forced herself to rise, to sit. To blink blearily into the whiteness of the sky.

She let out her breath and shook her head to clear the fuzziness.

She still took her pill at night.

She rose and padded to the bathroom, turned on the water, waited for it to get hot.

She stumbled into the hot stream. She noticed the caulk was getting grimy. She would need to rip it up and replace it. No point in calling the super.

It used to be a pain, coordinating everyone's showers so that there would be twenty-four hours for the caulk to dry.

"I can't not shower, Mom," Chloe would say. Sophie could hear her, clear as day. "That's like, totally gross."

If Jade were there, Chloe would have pointed a glance in Jade's direction, and Sophie would have narrowed her eyes to look disapproving.

Jade would have just smiled, then given Chloe the finger when she thought Sophie had turned back around.

Bob would have been just as bad. "I wish you would have told me you were planning to do this. I'm supposed to meet up with Tim and shoot a few rounds. Guess that's not going to happen now."

Now it would be easy.

She felt the hot tears on her face and raised her arms to hold the faucet and keep her knees from buckling.

She took a deep breath.

This is it, she told herself. *Stop this now. You have a job to get to.*

And, after a few minutes, it worked. She stopped trembling, steadied herself.

Rinsed out the rest of the shampoo.

And tried to keep her thoughts on the moment, right here: the fact that she was running five minutes late. For her first day back. She needed to shave her pits. Get dressed, brush her hair, put on makeup, do something so that her eyes didn't look red. Start the car. Make tea. Run a comb through the hair that had frozen when she went out to start the car.

Jade had left a note on the steering wheel. *Good Luck. C U 2nite.*

It was written in dark blue sharpie on the back of a McDonald's receipt. Sophie smoothed it out and placed it gently into her cupholder.

She drove slowly along the icy roads. She used to speed when she was late for work, then stop herself. *What would happen to Chloe without you?* she would think. Then she would slow down.

She never asked what would become of her without Chloe.

She shook her head, flinging the thought away.

Survival mode, she told herself. *Survival mode.*

It had taken hours to pack his things. Weeks before, he had come for the last of the furniture that was his, the forty-two-inch LCD. Now she had an old twenty-five-inch CRT. And the worn brown-and-tan sofa. And the whole bed to herself.

And nothing else.

She had expected to just wither away and die.

Instead, she had cleaned the apartment. Packed up Chloe's things. "You can stay here now," she told Jade, once they'd cleaned out Chloe's room.

Jade was still sleeping on the couch.

But she was staying more now. She might stay for two or three weeks, every night, then tell Sophie her mom wanted her back home. Sophie hoped it was true.

Jade had even spent most of Christmas there, marathoning cheesy B-movies, including a Canadian one about a murderous Santa defeated by a game of curling.

Now that Sophie had someone counting on a roof, she needed to pay the bills she'd been letting stack up. So she'd called her old boss and been shocked to hear they had waited for her.

She was not quite sure why she was doing it. Or how. She did not allow herself to feel any pride of accomplishment.

But here she was, pulling into the parking lot. Checking to make sure her hair looked OK, that none of her blouse buttons were undone.

Here she was, getting out of her car. Pushing through the doors. Smiling at the security guard.

Enduring their hugs. The smiles. The pitying looks.

Smiling through it all. Nodding. Telling them she just wanted to get back to work. That it would be good for her.

Telling herself that.

She slid behind her desk, finally.

Pressed the buttons to sign into her phone.

She took her first call. A modem issue. She found herself walking him through a reset without even thinking. It was easy, routine.

Her heart, racing from the morning's cup of tea, steadied.

She exhaled.

She would make it through the day.

She would not think about tomorrow.

March

Sophie was jerked from slumber by the sound of the phone ringing. It was Saturday morning, her day to sleep in. She thought about ignoring it, burrowing deeper beneath the warm covers, blocking out the relentless chill.

Then she looked at her phone and saw that it was Eddie.

"Hi," she breathed, barely even a whisper.

"How are you holding up?" he asked, not beating around the bush.

"Surviving," she whispered. Hearing the sound of his voice had sucked the air from her lungs.

"It fucking sucks," he said.

"Yes," she said.

"You want to grab drinks sometime?" he asked. "I . . . jeez . . . there's not anyone I can, you know—"

"Yes," she said.

They met up a week later at a pub. They sat facing each other in a cracked leather booth. They were near a window, and she pulled her fleece jacket tightly around herself to protect against the draft. She ordered a margarita; he ordered a beer.

He looked up at her, then back down to his drink. Then back up. "I don't even know what to say."

"It's been dark," she said. She'd meant to say, *It's been hard.*

"Yeah," he said. "I mean, I know I was a lousy father, but I loved her. So much. You have to believe me."

"I know," she said, meeting his eyes for the first time. They were dark blue pools. Chloe's eyes. "I know."

She thought that he really wasn't a bad father. Much better than Bob. Chloe had adored him. He just hadn't been around that much, living out of state for much of her childhood. Still, she hadn't known anything different. She hadn't missed him when he was gone.

Or Sophie hoped she hadn't. What kind of mother sets her daughter up for such pain? What kind of mother has a baby with someone who won't stick around?

She pushed the thoughts from her head. Their drinks arrived, and she took a long, cool sip. It had been a long time since she'd had alcohol, and she felt a burning sensation at the back of her throat.

Eddie downed half his beer in one long slurp. Some of it trickled down his broad, scruffy face. "Christ," he said, wiping a weather-worn hand through his beard. "What the hell are we supposed to do? Life isn't made for this kind of thing. You're supposed to walk them down the aisle and complain about the no-account hoodlum they're marrying, not bury them."

"Yes," she said. She stared at his hands, faded, calloused, the condensation from the glass trickling down them, little streaks of life.

He downed the rest of his beer. Ordered a second.

She, rather primly, took another sip of her margarita.

"Do you remember," he said, "when she was two or three, do you remember the way she couldn't say the word *truck*?"

"Yes." She expected to tear up, but instead found herself smiling. "And of course that was what you drove, and of course she was obsessed with it, so it was never *Daddy is here!* It was always *Daddy's fuck is here!*"

Eddie laughed then, and pounded on the table. Tears slid down the scruffy salt-and-pepper on his face.

She thought about how that line had always driven a dagger through her. For obvious reasons. It wasn't supposed to make her smile.

She took another sip from her drink. "Remember when she was obsessed with pink and princesses? And you were out of work, so you found one of the boys' action figures with long hair, and you made a tutu and one of those little crowns for it?"

He shook his head and chuckled. "It didn't look much like a tutu," he said. "More like, 'Inept man staples pink fabric.'"

"She loved it, though," Sophie said.

"Yeah." He looked down into the depths of his beer. "She was always so sweet. Didn't hardly take anything to make her happy."

"Can I ask you something?" she asked.

He looked up at her. Nodded.

She felt a pang, a stab. Those eyes.

"Is it easier," she asked, "because you have the boys? Is it any easier? To know that you still have them? That you are still a father?"

"No," he said. He took a long drink. "They don't care about me. I messed up, I don't know. I lost them somewhere in there. Chloe was the only one who still returned my calls. And now she's gone."

"But they're still here. You still have a chance."

He gave his head a shake. "Travis wrote me off a long time ago. David always picked up my calls. Let me buy him McDonald's. Lately, though . . . he just says he's busy. I hope he is. But I think he figured out what a lousy father I was." He sighed. "Wish I could do it all over again."

She felt her leg twitch.

Eddie ordered another beer.

"How's Bob?" he asked.

"I kicked him out in December."

"Good for you." His face cracked into a wide grin.

She jutted out her chin and sighed noticeably.

"No, I mean, sure, I hate to see you with anyone else, but, well . . . *Bob*. He was never any good for you. You need a man who sees how beautiful you are—what a great person you are. All that good stuff."

"All that good stuff."

"You know what I mean. Bob never acted like—he never acted like he knew what he had. Chloe didn't like him. Said he treated you both OK, but that he was an asshole."

"She was always a good judge of character." She wished, fleetingly, that she had kicked Bob out eons ago. And had that time, again, with Chloe. All to herself.

"Except for me," Eddie said. He grinned again. "She loved me a hell of a lot more than I deserved."

"Oh, you weren't so bad." She smiled. And finished her drink.

"You think I wasn't so bad, he must have messed up big. What did he do, anyway?"

She flushed. Pushed her index finger against the cracks in the faux leather seats. "I asked him if one day, maybe, we could have a baby. I know, I know, it is just me being stupid," she said without looking up. "I know she cannot be replaced.

I know it will not fix anything." She dipped her finger into the water beneath her glass and drew circles on the wood tabletop. "But I just wanted so badly to be a mother again. I wanted to think that maybe, maybe I could have that again. I do not know if that makes me naive or selfish or disrespectful or a horrible mother, but I just . . ."

He reached out and held her hand. "You were a wonderful mother," he said. "You will be again."

She lifted her head to meet his eyes. Dark and warm and welcoming. Shook her head.

"There's nothing wrong with you."

Tears welled in her eyes. She swallowed hard to force them down.

"Hell," he said. "You and me, we could make another baby. She'd be beautiful and god knows you'd raise her right. And I'd do better this time. Stick around, be involved."

"She wouldn't be Chloe," Sophie said. The tears spilled down her face.

It lay out there.

They ordered another round.

"We can't drive," she said as they stepped out into the chilly night air. She had never been one to drive after drinking, but it carried so much weight now.

"No," he said, "of course not. Your place is close by."

"OK," she said.

She felt like a teenager, tiptoeing past the living room where Jade was already asleep. It was thrilling.

Once inside her bedroom, he kissed her.

"I don't know," she said.

"You're beautiful," he said.

He ran a hand down her face. So softly.

His breath stunk of cheap beer and broken promises.

She looked around. Saw Chloe's ghost bouncing on the bed, dancing to the *Guardians of the Galaxy* soundtrack. Somersaulting across the floor. Squealing as she ran in from the doorway, phone in hand, having just been asked to homecoming.

"OK," she said. "OK."

They did not use condoms.

May

Sophie awoke to the smell of daffodils. Eddie had left the window open. The spring breeze was brisk, but the smells were heavenly. The sky was a brightening blue and cloudless.

She breathed deep.

She wiggled away from Eddie's arms and beer-soaked breath. She would be late for work.

On her way down the hall, she passed Chloe's door and wondered if she should start looking for a new place. She had cleaned the room, put everything away, but she still could not bear to open the door.

Images flooded her mind. Chloe at five, in a ballerina tutu, twirling in front of the mirror. Chloe at seven, leaping across the bed as her friend Kyra chased her. Chloe at eleven, curled over the cordless phone, whispering and giggling.

She shook her head. She should move away, find a new apartment without all of the memories. *No,* a voice told her, *you should stay*. After all, she was Chloe's mother. She was supposed to remember her. She was supposed to feel the pain. She was not supposed to get a new puppy, move on. She was not supposed to feel happy.

She was supposed to be a good mother.

But if she found a new place, Jade would have a room, a space. She deserved that. Last week, she'd had friends over, and Sophie had found it difficult to stay out of their way.

It had been odd, having Eddie's son here. There was something about his eyes that reminded her of Chloe.

He had tried to avoid looking at her.

"You can go in her room if you want," she'd told him. "There is a box of her things. If there is anything you want to keep, you can have it."

He had nodded, not saying anything.

Later on, he'd asked if he could have one of the photos, he and Chloe on a beach.

"Of course," she'd said.

"She was going to get rich and buy a house on the beach one day."

She remembered that. Chloe had drawn sketches of the house she wanted to build one day. "It was going to have a slide," she said.

"And a pool. And about a million other crazy things."

She was surprised that she hadn't broken down crying. "That was Chloe," she'd said. "Always a dreamer."

He had nodded then, and looked her in the eyes.

He looked so much like Chloe.

"You look like her," he said.

She hadn't realized it worked that way.

Jade had raised an eyebrow the first time she saw Eddie come padding out of Sophie's bedroom. Then smiled.

"You deserve to be happy," she'd told Sophie later.

Is this what that is? Sophie had wondered.

She brushed the taste of Eddie from her teeth.

She left him lying in bed while she went to work. She knew he would be gone when she returned. And she knew he would turn up, like a stray dog, whenever she opened her door.

She did not know if she was trying to erase Chloe or trying in vain to recreate her. She did not know which was worse.

But something had shifted. She found herself hoping they would replace the color printer at work. And thinking about maybe going up to the beach for a long weekend in the summer with Jade.

And she found herself thinking about other things, too.

Neutral colors.

Good second-hand stores.

Names.

9

BARE WITNESS

"Cassandra Marie Roberts, do you swear to tell the truth, the whole truth, and nothing but the truth?" My hand, outstretched, is resting on the Bible.

"Yes," I lie.

They have you swear on the Bible, before God, because they think it will work. People will worry less about the outcome of the trial and more about the eternal damnation of their souls.

But all that's lost on me.

I am a Heartless Bitch.

Once upon a time, four or five months ago, I believed in all of that Bible stuff, embodied it, felt it quiver through my soul. It's funny how quickly you can lose it all, how the foundation beneath your feet can slip away.

If you were looking in from the outside, you'd say it was the accident. *Oh, she went through the motions for a few months, but the accident made her angry at the world, made her question God.*

You'd be wrong.

It was a boy.

Or really, it was sex.

They taught me that it was a sin. *The* sin. Not my parents, but the church.

Not that they disagreed. It was something they pretty much all agreed on—church, school, my parents: Don't have sex.

My parents taught me that sex was stupid. They'd had sex —not even in high school, they were smart and reasonable and waited until college—and look what happened. They had been stupid, they said.

No, I thought to myself, *you were punished*.

"You're not a punishment," Mrs. DeLuca had told me once. *Amanda*, as she had repeatedly instructed me to call her. Matt's mom. "Children are a gift."

It was poison, those things she told me. Things that made me think I should be more like her, more like *Amanda*. Free and easy.

I try to push her from my mind.

It's hard; she is sitting just in front of me, next to the bearded lawyer in the blue suit. Looking at me.

They are all looking at me.

My parents held sex out as "The Thing You Could Do To Ruin Your Life." Worse than getting a B, or even an F. Worse than drinking, worse than drugs. Worse than wrecking your car.

They were supposed to be a doctor and a lawyer.

Instead, they were just my mom and dad.

Sex could screw up your whole life.

It turned out they were wrong. Not nagging your friend to buckle her seat belt could screw up your whole life.

"I don't like you dating," my mother said.

So I told her Matt and I were just friends. He was on the honor roll too. We were working on a project together.

"You shouldn't be alone in your room with a boy," my father said. "Even if he is just a friend."

So I let Matt in through my window, where my parents couldn't see.

I wasn't rebelling, breaking all the rules, going bad.

I just knew better than them. That I was strong enough, stubborn enough. I didn't need their rules to protect me.

"They want to control you," Mrs. DeLuca (*Amanda*) had said when I'd told her they didn't want me dating. "They think they veered off their paths and screwed up their lives, and so they want to make sure you don't do the same. Which I get, but . . . you can't ever control your kids, not really. They have their own paths to follow, their own mistakes to make. They want to save you from the pain, but . . . well, that's life."

"I can control myself," I told her. "I don't need to make mistakes. I can look around me; I'm not dumb." I took a lot of pride in that. I could make my own rules, and I could follow them. Trig homework before dinner, doesn't matter how hungry you are. Five pages of the term paper before bed, doesn't matter how tired you are. Don't let the boyfriend into your pants, doesn't matter how horny you are.

My parents hadn't wanted me to get a car. They thought I wouldn't have enough money for college. Or that I'd be stuck working to pay for it and wouldn't have enough time for school and extracurriculars. Or that I'd crash it.

If it were just my parents, I probably would have had sex six months earlier, the first time I sensed Matt wanted to. *Birth control has come a long way*, I would have rationalized. But my parents had God on their side.

My parents weren't big on church, but I loved it there. At church, the adults didn't care if I got a B. They didn't care if I kept my room spotless or was always punctual or took the right internship or socialized with "the right people."

There was just one thing, this one thing they wanted you to do: Save yourself.

Save yourself for marriage.

It reinforced everything I had always been taught.

And it helped me realize that my parents were sinners. And that I could be better, not in grades or transcripts, but where it counted. I could be right with the Lord.

We talked about it almost every week at youth group, in one form or another. The fact that pre-marital sex was evil was never contested, we just debated the proper way to avoid temptation. We talked about the pressures facing kids, the unrealistic images we saw on our television sets. The temptations that were all around us. We signed pledges; we wore rings. We practiced saying no to one another.

"C'mon, baby," Chloe said to me in husky voice. "Show how much you love me."

"I love you enough not to let you make this mistake," I recited. "If you love me half as much, you'll wait for me."

Chloe giggled. "C'mon, who says that?" she asked. "What would you really say? If I were Matt?"

I looked up and met her eyes. "I'd say no," I told her. "I'd say, *You know I can't*."

"OK," she said, looking away. "I believe you."

I wonder if she did.

"You may be seated."

I sit, staring past the balding district attorney in the gray suit, the crowd behind him a blur of color. He smiles slightly at me. He thinks we're on the same side.

It's a Wednesday in May, barely a month until finals. I should be in school. Instead, I am here. An excused absence.

I would give anything to be in school right now.

"What was your relationship with the victim, Miss Chloe Moraru?"

"She was my best friend." The word *was* used to get me. Used to make me bite the inside of my cheek, then force a crooked smile, part of my cheek jutting inward, clamped between my teeth. *Can't let them see you cry.*

Now I am OK. Now I just dig my fingernails into the arms of the wooden chair and take a deep breath.

One Saturday night in January, long after Chloe had died and the world had gone to hell, Matt was in my room, crying, and then I was kissing him, and then he was taking off my shirt and I was undoing his jeans, and then he was reaching to undo mine.

I am not going to say that one thing led to another. There was a moment, I remember it distinctly, as his jeans were dropping to the floor, where I thought, *We are going to have sex.* And while some part of my head was screaming, *No, stop, wait!* my body just kept playing along.

Matt and I hadn't been the same since the accident. I wanted to reach my arms through the black void that stretched between us, unremarked upon, and pull him back to me, or maybe pull myself through the void, the dark emptiness, the unknown, and back to him.

He was crying, and I wanted to comfort him. I held him in my arms, I kissed him, told him that I loved him. And none of it helped, so I peeled off his shirt, hunter green and smelling of Old Spice and a faint, almost pleasant body odor. I threw out the suggestion, all the time telling myself that I didn't really mean it.

But when he took off my shirt, I didn't protest. Instead, I undid his Levi's button and dragged the zipper down along the bulge in his pants.

And when he undid my jeans, I helped him. I slid my hands along my thighs to wiggle out of them, taking my underwear with them as well.

I left my ring on.

Afterward, my insides raw, I smiled at him, breathed in

deep the cottony scent of his hair. I told him that I loved him. I told myself I had never felt closer to him. I lay with my head pressed against his chest and listened to his heart thump.

We were as close as any two human beings could get, pressed up against each other beneath my sheets, naked, our sweat sticking our skin together.

Upstairs, my parents slept.

I did not go to church the next morning.

It wasn't shame. No, I felt betrayed.

I'd had sex. The be-all, end-all of teenage existence. My dance with the devil; my fall from grace.

Except it wasn't any of those things. It was making out, with a little something new. Fitting my body against someone else's, trying to give us both pleasure.

It was nothing.

It was nothing wrong.

My parents were right—the only reason to fear sex was a baby. And that was hardly eternal damnation. It could even be something beautiful.

Regardless, Matt had used a condom.

The church had lied to me.

"Can you tell me about the day Chloe died?"

It's the lawyer. The one in the gray suit. The one who is supposed to be on my side.

Or really, I am supposed to be on his side.

Another breath. I look for Matt in the crowd.

He is seated in the second row, beside his father, behind his mother. He is wearing a black shirt and a gray coat, no tie. His brown hair flops across his face as I try to meet his eyes.

He looks back at me, eyes wide. Are they pleading?

. . .

I never blamed God for Chloe's death. Maybe I should've, but I didn't. I went to church more, prayed more, hoped God would make everything better.

Instead, I blamed the other driver.

Mrs. DeLuca.

Amanda.

Matt's mother.

I blamed her for thinking she could have a few margaritas and then pick her daughter up from school. I blamed her for blasting through the intersection. I blamed her for not noticing me.

I blamed Matt for being her son, and for staying after school to use the darkroom for so long that Jenna, his sister, got sick of waiting and called their mother for a ride. I blamed Jenna, for being impatient, and for not noticing that her mother was drunk, or if she did notice, for not taking away her keys the way they always taught you to at those *very special* assemblies.

And I blamed myself, for driving the car that Chloe was in, for not yelling at her to buckle up, for not seeing the SUV steaming toward us, for not reacting in time once I did see it. And for every time I'd ever smiled at or talked to Mrs. DeLuca, every nice thing I'd ever said to or thought about her. For sipping the wine she poured us at New Year's, for going to Six Flags with Matt's family last summer, for once upon a time wishing that my mother could be more like her.

At first I didn't talk to him. It was too hard, too painful.

He tried calling. I ignored his texts. He didn't come to the funeral and I blamed him. For picking sides.

I expected him to get pissed and go silent. That was what we did. Only this time, I wouldn't chase him.

But I came back to school and he hung out near my locker. And waited, every morning.

I ignored him.

Then Kyra and I stopped speaking and I got lonely.

I just don't want to talk about any of it, I texted Matt. *Can we do that?*

He texted back: *Yes*.

After that, we danced on eggshells.

Then his mom moved out in December, and in January he found out his dad had moved on and that neither of them had any intention of trying to fix things. And he came over and broke all of our rules and talked about all of it. And I had sex with him.

It was messed up; I know that, of course I know that. But what wasn't? If sex fixed things, even just a little bit, then so what?

And it did fix things. That was the miracle. After that, we could talk about his family. And about Chloe. And all the other things gummed up between us. We were close, as close as two people could be.

He was my person. I didn't need the church, I didn't need my parents, I didn't need my friends.

I just needed Matt, this one person, to truly see me. And love me.

The lawyer is waiting for me, smiling patiently. *This first part will be easy*, I tell myself. I rub my hands across my thighs, try not to fidget. Keep the lawyer in my periphery, my focus on Matt, the deep brown of his eyes.

I love him. I can do this for him.

"We were leaving school," I say. "I had a Key Club meeting, so it was about four thirty when we got to the car. Chloe was going to sit up front, but the new girl, Lacey, she needed a ride, so Chloe moved to the back seat. With our other friend, Kyra."

Kyra and I still aren't speaking. I think she slept with Chloe's boyfriend last fall. Just a few months after Chloe died.

She thinks I am a Heartless Bitch who drove the car that killed our best friend. So it is mutual.

Don't let them see you crack.

Lacey was never our friend, and now avoids us, no doubt blaming herself for taking Chloe's seat, for being alive while Chloe is dead. She hangs out with the burnouts now. I should feel bad, but here's where being a Heartless Bitch comes in. I'm just glad I don't have to see her very often.

"Which side of the back seat did she sit on?"

"Driver's side," I say. "Behind me."

"Can you tell me, in your own words, what happened?"

I force myself to focus on Matt, the sadness pooled in his eyes.

This is what we practiced for, at the DA's office. There are two versions of this story; there is the truth, and there is the one I am about to give.

Matt brought it up last month, after sex, while I was laying naked against his chest once again, plastered to him, listening to the steady rhythm of his heartbeat.

"Maybe you could say you don't remember," he whispered. His heart seemed to speed up, *thum-thum, thum-thum, thum-thum*.

He had been worrying about the trial, about his mother going to jail. About how she would survive in there, what would happen to his already decaying family, how his sister was going to fall apart, and so on.

I had been trying to tell him it would all be OK; secretly wishing he would talk about something else. I wanted his mother to go to jail. She deserved to be in jail.

Maybe you could say you don't remember. He let it hang there for an eternity, its shadow making me suddenly feel very naked, very exposed.

"I mean, how well do you really remember?" he finally

said, breaking the silence, talking way too fast. "Are you sure you looked before you turned? Are you sure she wasn't there?

"I'm not saying it's your fault; I know it wasn't your fault."

I wondered if he did.

"I know she shouldn't have been drinking. *She* knows she shouldn't have been drinking. But maybe it's just nobody's fault. Maybe it's just one of those things. She made a mistake, yeah, but if she wasn't speeding or doing anything reckless, then it wasn't really her fault either. I mean, she doesn't deserve to go to jail for it. My sister doesn't deserve to lose her mother over it. Maybe it was just an accident."

I am a cold and Heartless Bitch, so I don't care. And it was not just an accident.

"She loved you, you know?" he continued. "And you loved her. I know you did. You came over to hang out even when I wasn't home. You loved my family. How can you just turn that off? How can you just abandon us?"

She killed my best friend, Matt. That's how.

"Maybe it was nobody's fault. Maybe you could forgive her."

The church had been big on forgiveness.

I sidestepped the issue. "Forgiveness isn't the same as lying," I said.

His heart stopped. Then started again.

"But how much do you really remember?" he asked. "It was seven months ago. Are you 100 percent sure of what you saw? Sure enough to destroy her life, my sister's life, my life?"

I looked up at him and his eyes were pleading.

"She's gotten better. No more drinking, trying to be, I don't know, like she was before. She's already been rehabilitated. What the hell good does it do anyone for her to go to jail?"

I said nothing.

"Could you just do it for me?"

When I said nothing, Matt dropped his head and cried into my hair.

I felt his tears, warm and slick, seep down the side of my face.

I thought about how poetic this was, like I was crying his tears. Me, the girl who couldn't cry her own tears. His tears running down my face. And me, the Heartless Bitch, feeling everything he felt.

I wanted, more than anything, for him to be happy. Matt, lying naked before me. The only person left in the world who I loved.

And then I told my first lie. "I think," I said, "I can forgive her."

And he wrapped his arms around me and kissed the back of my neck.

And I shifted, ever so slightly, against his chest, so I could no longer hear the slow, steady, *thum-thum* of his heart.

The gray-suited DA moves in front of me, blocking my view of Matt. I move my head back and forth, but I am stuck, staring at the gray suit.

On the other side of the aisle, I see Pastor Rick, my former minister. From back when I used to believe in things.

I look away from him. I look at the DA, study the red stripes on his tie. I wonder who decided that stripes on ties must be diagonal.

"We were at the intersection in front of the school," I finally say. This much is still safe. "We had to make a left." I speak as slowly as possible, try to drag this out. "There was another car that was coming—they didn't have a stop sign— and they plowed into us while we were turning."

"Did you see this car?"

And here it is, the moment of truth. If I didn't see her,

then she was speeding. Then she was at fault. If I did see her, and I turned anyway, or if I didn't look . . . then I was at fault.

I look at Matt and he is looking at me. Right in my eyes. Seeing my soul. Nodding at me. His breath held. His life, his happiness, in my hands.

"I love you," he always says, right after we finish.

I lay there naked and vulnerable. "I love you, too," I whisper back.

I don't even know who I am anymore.

I want to reach out, across the room, and run my hands through his hair, across his cheek. I want to kiss him and tell him everything will be OK. That I will not let him down. That I will be the one person in this crazy world he can count on.

"I don't remember," I try to say, but it sticks at the back of my throat.

I find myself remembering a Sunday school session, a year or two ago. Chloe was there, sitting next to me, like she always was. Like she was always supposed to be.

"This is the story that always bugged me," Pastor Rick was saying. "God asks Abraham to sacrifice his son. And Abraham goes to do it. Sure, God stops him in the nick of time, but why ask such a thing in the first place? What kind of a loving God would ask a father to sacrifice his son? What kind of a loving father would agree?"

"It's stupid," I remember Chloe saying. She was always more willing to question things than me; always more willing to thrust out her opinion. "I think Abraham sucks for going along with it."

I leaned away from Chloe, turning my head toward the boy sitting next to me, but Pastor Rick nodded. "I agree," he said. "When I heard that story, I thought, *No way. God ever asks me to kill my child, no way. He is my Lord and Savior, but I'd rather go to hell."*

We all stared at him. There were about seven of us, I think. I don't know if we were more shocked by the sentiment or just the word—hell—coming from our minister's mouth.

"But I thought about it a lot," he said. "Because it bothered me. And here's what I think. I don't think it's any accident he doesn't say *kill*. He says *sacrifice*. I think it's a metaphor."

I nodded, ever the good Sunday school student. Of course it was a metaphor. They were all metaphors.

"When we talk about God, what is it that we say to our secular brothers and sisters? To spread the word to them in a language they'll understand?"

"The greater good," I said quickly, before anyone else could answer.

"That's really all the Bible is about. Making sacrifices for the greater good of all mankind."

"So it's OK to kill your child, if it saves five others?" Chloe asked, eyes narrowed.

I wonder now, had she lived, how long it would have taken her to question everything. Would she, like me, lose faith one day?

"Probably," he said. "I can't say I'd do that. Practicing what you preach is always the hardest part." He peered down from behind his glasses and smiled at her. "Let's try an easier example. It's midnight. My son comes home covered in blood. Won't talk about it. Two hours later, the police appear at my door. They ask me if my son's been home all night. What should I say?"

"You tell the truth," I answered.

"But maybe it was an accident," he said. "Maybe he did nothing wrong. I want to protect him . . . you might not understand this yet, but when you have children, you feel it so strongly. You have been given a precious life, and it is your duty to protect this life, even with your own."

"You still have to tell them," I argued. I, too, could be argumentative, if I knew I was right.

"Yes," he said. I was vindicated. "You know why?"

"It's the right thing to do."

"But why?"

Silence filled the room.

"Because that's what you'd want them to do," Chloe said, "if it was the other way around. Maybe your kid's the one who's hurt or dead. You would want to find the person who did it. You would want to know the truth."

"Exactly!" He jabbed a finger in her direction. "That's what the sacrifice is about. You have to lay the people you love upon the rock, hold them up to the world. If everyone protected their own, we would have no justice, no protection from those who seek to do us harm. It's for the greater good that we must let go, that we must speak the truth, even when it pains us to do so. Even when it hurts the ones we hold closest."

The DA repeats the question. "Did you see the other car?" He is skinny, too young to be going bald.

And yet he is.

I see Chloe's mother, Sophie. A couple of kids from school sit next to her; I think one of them is Chloe's brother.

I don't want to look at Sophie, but I do. Her eyes are closed; her lower lip is clamped between her teeth. I wonder, for a moment, if she is praying.

It won't do her any good, I remind myself. The truth will hurt Matt. It will hurt Mrs. DeLuca. And Chloe will still be dead.

The DA moves then, shifts to the right, and I can see

Mrs. DeLuca. She is bent, her head down. She looks so small from up here. So drained of her usual joy.

He shifts some more and I see Matt again. Looking at me. Mouth moving. Is he praying? Is he begging me?

I think about the feel of his fingers on my face, caressing my cheek. I think about the way he smells, like earth and grass and sweat, and how warm he is pressed against my body.

The world's gone to hell, he told me once. *I can't count on my parents anymore. You're the only person I can count on. The only person I trust.*

I open my mouth.

"Did you see the other car?"

I try to say the words, the ones Matt wants me to say, but they stick. *Not even a lie*, I'd told myself. *An omission*. But I can't do it.

So I fall back on the other word, the one I practiced in the DA's office, the one I practiced all my life, the one I could never quite say to Matt.

"No."

The earth shifts. I don't look at Matt, but I feel the change from *us* to *me*. Like I was holding our collective breaths, and I exhaled, and he is gone.

"Did you look?" the DA asks.

I do not hesitate now. "Yes. The road was clear. The other car just came out of nowhere." In my head, it's a snapshot. A clear road, cars stopped at the light at the corner. The world frozen, everything OK. It's the first image in my head every morning.

The next thing that comes to me is always a sudden jerk of my head, the sound of breaking glass, the feel of everything turning sideways, and then the relief that it was over, and we were all OK. Then the throbbing in my nose. Then the screaming.

Matt's gaze drops. He rests his forehead on the bench in front of him. His father rubs his back. He is shaking.

I want to cry.

Don't break. Don't ever break.

"Then what happened?"

I breathe in. Breathe out.

Mrs. DeLuca is looking down at her lap, knotting her hands together.

"You're an amazing kid," I remember her saying to me once, for no particular reason at all. "Your parents should be proud."

I look away.

I look for Chloe's mother again, but her head is now buried in her hands.

I find Kyra. She sits beside her father, chewing on her lower lip. Our eyes meet, and she stares at me. Her eyes are dark and round and piercing.

I have been a horrible friend.

I swallow. "I made the turn. Most of it. Then there were these squealing tires . . . I saw the SUV out of the corner of my eye, but there was nothing I could do. I tried to speed up, I think. It didn't matter. It hit right where Chloe was sitting. She hit the window. With her head."

"And then what happened?"

Kyra keeps looking at me, her legs shaking slightly, up and down, up and down, like they do while she's at a basketball game, waiting for her chance to play. I pretend she is urging me on.

"There were a lot of voices, and screaming. I hit my face against the steering wheel. Broken nose, lots of blood. I think I was just panicking for a minute or two. Everything hurt. The screaming. I didn't know if I was hurt badly. But I started to get my head together. I was able to push myself up, look around."

"What did you see?"

"Lacey was sitting next to me. She looked fine. She actually got out of the car. So I knew she was OK."

Kyra's gaze is still fixed on me. I even imagine that I see her nod.

"I tried to look behind me, which was hard. I had to undo the seat belt—it had locked up, choking me almost. I had to put my feet against the window, twist around in my seat."

I swallow.

"Kyra was right behind Lacey. She was screaming and cursing and holding her leg. She was OK."

"And Chloe?"

"Chloe wasn't saying anything," I say. "She was on top of her, on top of Kyra. Practically crushing her."

Kyra's eyes squint, tight. I think I see her swallow.

If I had only yelled at her to buckle up . . . but she was going to, she was just getting situated, checking her phone; we were hardly out of the parking lot.

"Her head—her hair . . . she had really curly dark hair. And there was all this blood in it, and going down the side of her face."

"Did she say anything?" he asks. But he already knows the answer.

"No," I say. "But her eyes were open."

Kyra keeps looking at me. She is sitting near the back of the courtroom, but I can see her chest moving up and down, up and down. I know she wants to stop looking, to close her eyes. But she keeps them on me.

"When did you find out Chloe was dead?" he asks.

"Later," I say, running a knuckle up and down my nose. "Maybe an hour later. At the hospital. They tried to operate, but it didn't work. I was sitting with her mom when the doctor came in."

I think about Chloe's mom, pressed against me, as I tried to hold her up, of the way it felt to fall as she pulled me to the floor. I see her stepfather, face red, struggling for air. I see her angry stepsister's face contort. I see Chloe's stoner younger brother run past me, a blur. I see her older brother in the back of the room, looking like me. Lips pressed together, eyes wide, blinking. Swallowing. Shaking.

"No further questions," he says.

"Your witness," the judge says.

The other lawyer, the enemy, bearded and in a blue suit. He looks me up and down.

"The day of the accident," he says, stroking his beard. "How long had you had your license?"

I see Kyra's jaw clench. *Them's fighting words.*

I remain calm and steady, like I practiced. "Three weeks."

"And you say you didn't see the car."

"No," I say. It is easier now.

"You looked?"

"Yes."

"You remember this, all those months back?"

"Yes." I am starting to get annoyed with him.

"It's OK if you didn't," he says. "You were young, it was an accident. What would be tragic," he looks to the jury, "would be to send a woman to prison, a mother of two, for what was just an accident."

I see Kyra's father's hand on her shoulder. Holding her down.

"I looked," I say, trying to keep the irritation from my voice. "Kyra was giving me a hard time, I think she said something like, *Can we just get out of here already?* And I remember Chloe said to her, *Maybe that's why you failed drivers ed.* Chloe could be kind of snarky like that. And I took my time, just to, I don't know, just to make her wait longer. To be a little bit of a bitch, I guess."

Kyra smiles at that admission. A few tears streak across her lips, but she smiles.

I continue. "I looked left; I looked right. There was no one there. Then I turned."

Kyra is nodding at me.

The attorney pauses, hand frozen, tugging on that beard.

Mrs. DeLuca's head drops to her lap.

"OK," the lawyer says finally, hand dropping from his beard. "I just have a few more questions."

After the gavel pounded.

At night, at home.

In the bathroom.

I turn the shower on.

I stare at the mirror.

I slide out of my jacket. Let it hit the floor.

It will need to be ironed.

Unbutton my shirt.

Unbutton the cuffs at my wrists.

Slide it off my shoulders, let it hit the floor.

Unzip the side of my skirt, let it fall.

Kick off the heels, peel off the pantyhose, the underwear.

Unhook the bra and let it slide down my arms.

Naked.

Alone this time.

I stare at the mirror as it fogs.

I think about Matt's kitchen. Sitting at the island. Matt next to me, chewing a sandwich. Mrs. DeLuca, *Amanda*, leaning on the other side, her wavy hair loose and messy. I am complaining about my parents. How they hate that I am buying a car. The things they say to me, the little digs, how they tell me I will just lose my job, then the car, then my credit rating. That I'll never save enough for college now. Or that I'll crash it.

I do everything perfect, straight As, church every Sunday, youth group every Wednesday, Key Club every Tuesday, work every other day. And they have no faith in me.

"I think they're jealous," she is telling me, swirling an olive in her drink. "They share a car, don't they?"

"Yes," I say. I am munching on the Doritos she laid out.

Cool Ranch, which neither of her kids like, bought specifi-cally for me. "But this is my money. And I'm still setting a bunch aside for college. I can't keep relying on Matt to drive me to work, or walking two miles in the snow. I can pick up extra shifts this way."

"I think you're making a smart decision," she says. "You know your parents. They wanted so much more. When they see you using this to better yourself, and saving just as much as you always have, they'll come around."

"They make everything so hard," I say. I hold my face in my hands. I know I am whining, but I don't really care. "I get an A, and it should have been in an AP class. I make a hundred dollars in tips, and I should have taken that unpaid internship at that law office when I don't even want to be a lawyer. Then I go to spend some of the money, and I shouldn't, because all of a sudden it's important that I be saving money. Which I wouldn't even have if I had taken the internship."

"I know," she says. "I think they're trying to live through you, and it's just causing a lot of pain all around. They put too much on you." She sips her drink. "I think it will be easier when you move out. You might like them, when you don't have to live with them."

I say nothing.

"Or you might not," she says. "But I think it will all be easier when you have a little distance."

I remember nodding, making sure to tuck that nugget away. *It's wise,* I thought. I would remember it one day and think it was really wise.

I liked her.

I snap the barettes out of my hair; let it fall down across my face frizzy and wild.

I remember her dancing in the living room to Bowie, hair flying around her face.

I picture the guards shaving it in jail, the beautiful blond tresses, though I'm pretty sure that only happens in the movies, and only to hard criminals.

I hold my breath and hold my face and keep the tears from falling until I am safely in the shower, until they can be washed away.

Until I can be wiped clean.

She'll probably do sixty days, the DA said. Sixty days can be forever. Or nothing. Sixty days and the debt is paid, the slate is clean.

Does it really work like that?

I sit on the bathtub floor. Outside, the sun is setting, and the room is growing dark.

It's the damnedest thing, but I don't think about Chloe, or even Matt. I think about Amanda, lying in bed shivering, back to the gray concrete wall, eyes fixed, untrusting, on her roommate's bed. Waiting until she can relax, waiting for it all to get better.

And I remember her laugh, the way it lilted through the room, the way it used to make me smile, the way it made me dream. I would marry Matt, I would get his family; I would become part of that warm, happy bubble.

I had loved her. I had loved Matt more, but still. I loved his mother too.

I sit in the dark, the water running cold.

I wonder if this is what forgiveness feels like.

THE BEGINNING

This is what it looks like:
  Shaking fingers
  Pursed lips
  A plastic wand
  A whispered prayer
  One pink line
  Then another
  A smile, broad and rippling
  Then
  Knees buckling
  Face cracking
  Linoleum beneath her hands
  Footsteps
  The girl who is almost her daughter
  Holds her from behind
  It will be OK, it will be OK
  It is an excruciating blessing
  He will never know his sister

ACKNOWLEDGMENTS

Thanks, first and foremost, to my family. Chris, my first reader, my champion, the love of my life. Thank you for believing in me. Thank you for reading little pieces of my soul and treating them with care and love. Thank you for dragging me into our writers' group. Thank you for saying the one thing that helped me fix so many of the problems with my first draft. Thank you for doing the thousands of things you do every day to keep my life easy (school drop-offs and pickups, cleaning the stupid bathrooms, hitting seven different stores to find the one particular type of lemonade I like, etc). For making me laugh. For your sad happy dance. For letting me over plan vacations and under plan school lunch. For nurturing my love of board games (and winning). For (finally) acknowledging that mountain isn't manly. For getting me. For being my person.

Thank you to Phoenix, without whom this book would have never been possible, for being the best, coolest kid in the world. I wrote chapters of this book with you as an infant, asleep against my chest. You crashed on the couch while I frantically rearranged and re-wrote a chunk of the novel in one night. Thank you for (sort of) understanding when I glue myself to a computer instead of playing with Legos. For loving good books and great music. For forcing me out into the world. For being an awesome person. For making being a parent (mostly) fun. For having a precocious sense of humor and fantastic political skills. For always championing the side characters.

Thanks to my parents, for encouraging me to follow my dreams. For not batting an eye when I turned down a free ride to the local college instead go away to Art school. For helping buy my first laptop, for believing in me when I didn't believe in myself. For all of the endless babysitting.

Thanks to my brother, Ryan Boluyt, for being my first audience and always going along with my characters when we'd play. For knowing how to tempt my teenage self into having family dinner ("food and political debate"), for always accepting me unconditionally. For helping me buy my first laptop, for putting up with me, and moving back to Michigan (that was totally because you missed me, right?). For being not just a brother, but a great friend.

Thank you to Evelyn Eberline (and Adam, Adelina, Arabella, and Alcide), for being my other family. For always being there when I need you and giving the best advice. For listening to me ramble on, for putting up with my overplanning, for never rolling your eyes when I am inevitably late. For always promising me everything was going to be okay, and for always, somehow, being right.

Thank you to my brother-in-law, Mark Vorenkamp, for your early reading and astute feedback.

Thanks to the Chelsea Writers' Workshop and the Longer

Works group, particularly Brian Cox, Meg Gower, and Michael Kitchen. For making my writing good, making it a little less "actively hostile to the reader" (still love that quote), for reading multiple revisions, and for encouraging (some would say forcing) me to do something with it. I could not have done this without you guys.

Thanks to all the teammates I've worked with over the years at Borders, ADP, and Michigan Medicine - I have been blessed to work with some amazing people, and your encouragement and friendship has made shy, insecure me into the semi-confident, people-loving person I am today.

Thank you to my editor, Lara Zielin, for pushing this Novel to be better. Thanks for your advice and patience, your astute eye for the things that didn't quite work, and your amazing Novel summary.

Thank you to the Fifth Avenue Press for guiding me through this process and bringing this story to life. It's been an amazing journey.

ABOUT THE AUTHOR

Shanelle O. Boluyt grew up in Dexter, Michigan. After spending her teenage years swearing she would get as far away from home as possible, she landed...one town over, in Chelsea, Michigan, where she lives with her husband, son, and cat. A graduate of the Fiction Writing program at Columbia College Chicago, she serves as the IT Director for the Chelsea Writers' Workshop. *Intersections* is her debut novel.